Napoleon Dynamite
FINAL SHOOTING SCRIPT

FINAL SHOOTING SCRIPT FOR THE HIT FILM
FROM FOX SEARCHLIGHT PICTURES
WRITTEN BY JARED HESS AND JERUSHA HESS

SIMON SPOTLIGHT ENTERTAINMENT
New York   London   Toronto   Sydney

Historian's Note: This is the final shooting script for the film *Napoleon Dynamite*; thus we have preserved any typos and misattributions. The script may include dialogue or even full scenes that were not in the final version of the film. Also, there may be elements in the film that were added at a later date.

SSE

SIMON SPOTLIGHT ENTERTAINMENT
An imprint of Simon & Schuster Children's Publishing Division
1230 Avenue of the Americas, New York, New York 10020
© 2006 Twentieth Century Fox Film Corporation and
Paramount Pictures Corporation. All Rights Reserved.
All rights reserved, including the right of reproduction in
whole or in part in any form.
SIMON SPOTLIGHT ENTERTAINMENT and related logo are trademarks
of Simon & Schuster, Inc.
Designed by Yaffa Jaskoll
Manufactured in the United States of America
10 9 8 7 6 5 4 3 2
Library of Congress Control Number 2005938674
ISBN-13: 978-1-4169-2766-2
ISBN-10: 1-4169-2766-2

NAPOLEON DYNAMITE

Written by
Jared Hess and Jerusha Hess

FOX SEARCHLIGHT PICTURES ACQUISITION

FINAL SHOOTING SCRIPT
April 25, 2003

Napoleon Dynamite

by
Jared Hess
&
Jerusha Hess

04/25/2003

EXT. NAPOLEON'S HOUSE - MORNING

NAPOLEON, a high school teenager, stands in front of his small farmhouse waiting for the school bus. He has curly, poufy hair with bed-head, generic glasses, early 90s moon boots, and a t-shirt with an Idaho wildlife scene printed on it.

He opens his Trapper Keeper to reveal an action figure attached to some fishing line. A school bus screeches to a halt in front of him. He closes the Trapper Keeper.

INT. SCHOOL BUS - MORNING

The bus door opens. Napoleon gets on and goes to the very back. He sits down next to VERN, a kindergartner eating a hash-brown.

                    VERN
     What are you gonna do today Napoleon?

                    NAPOLEON
     Whatever I feel like I wanna do, gosh!

Napoleon opens the window next to him and takes out his action figure. He looks ahead to make sure the BUS DRIVER isn't watching. He wraps more fishing line around the action figure and then chucks it out the window.

EXT. SCHOOL BUS - MORNING

The action figure is being dragged behind the bus.

INT. SCHOOL BUS - MORNING

Napoleon watches the action figure. He makes a fist and jerks it down.

                    NAPOLEON
     Yes!

EXT. SCHOOL BUS - MORNING

The action figure is still being dragged.

INT. HIGH SCHOOL CLASSROOM - DAY

Napoleon sits at his desk drawing a picture of
a warrior holding a battle ax. A GIRL is reading
a current event.

                     GIRL
          . . . the United Nations will continue
          its relief efforts to hurricane
          victims in Roatan.

The girl sits down behind Napoleon.

                    TEACHER
          Napoleon, your current event?

Napoleon pulls out a tabloid article with a
picture of the Loch Ness monster on it. He
walks to the front of the class.

                    NAPOLEON
          Last week Japanese scientists placed
          explosive detonators at the bottom of
          the lake Loch Ness to blow Nessie out
          of the water.

                     RANDY
          Bullcrap Napoleon.

Napoleon stops reading. Beat.

                    NAPOLEON
          Sir Court Godfrey of the Nessie
          Alliance summoned the help of
          Scotland's local Wizards to cast a
          protective spell so -

                                                    2

                    RANDY
        Oh yeah right.

                    NAPOLEON
        Randy why don't you go find your
        grandma or something you're bugging
        the heck out of me, gosh!

INT. HIGH SCHOOL HALLWAY - DAY

Randy holds Napoleon in a headlock in front of
his locker. They struggle.

INT. HIGH SCHOOL LOCKER ROOM - DAY

Napoleon sits apart from a group of JOCKS all
dressed in P.E. clothes. Napoleon puts his moon
boots on.

                    DON
        Hey, Napoleon what did you do all
        summer again?

                    NAPOLEON
        I told you, I spent it with my uncle
        in Alaska hunting wolverines!

                    DON
        Did you shoot any?

                    NAPOLEON
        Yes! Like fifty of 'em. They kept
        trying to attack my cousins! What the
        heck would you do in a situation like
        that?

                    DON
        What kind of gun did you use?

                    NAPOLEON
        A freakin' twelve gauge, whadya think!

EXT. HIGH SCHOOL BASKETBALL COURT - DAY

A group of BOYS play basketball. A group of
GIRLS play jump rope. Napoleon plays tether-
ball by himself.

INT. HIGH SCHOOL OFFICE - DAY

Napoleon walks to a desk in an office. A
SECRETARY sits typing.

                    NAPOLEON
          Hey, could I use yer guyses phone for
          a sec?

                    SECRETARY
          Who do you need to call?

                    NAPOLEON
          My grandma.

                    SECRETARY
          Is there anything wrong?

                    NAPOLEON
          I don't feel very good.

The Secretary hands the phone over the desk.
Napoleon grabs the phone, dials and turns
around shielding himself from the Secretary.

INT. NAPOLEON'S LIVING ROOM - DAY

A phone rings on a kitchen counter. Beat. KIP,
a small, thin man in his late twenties wearing
big glasses, a polo buttoned to the top,
tapered jeans, a clean cut mustache, and a
conservative part in his hair, holds a brick of
cheddar. He shreds it over a plate of chips.
Kip answers the phone.

                         KIP
          Hello?

                       NAPOLEON
          Is grandma there?

                         KIP
          No she's getting her hair done.

                       NAPOLEON
          Ahhhhhhhh!

                         KIP
          Whadya need?

                       NAPOLEON
          Ahhhhh. Can you just go get her for
          me?

                         KIP
          I'm busy right now.

                       NAPOLEON
          Well just tell her to come get me.

                         KIP
          Why?

                       NAPOLEON
          Cuz I don't feel good!

                         KIP
          Did you talk to the school nurse?

                       NAPOLEON
          No. She doesn't know anything!

     Beat.

INT. HIGH SCHOOL OFFICE - DAY

                    NAPOLEON
          Will you just come get me?

                    KIP

          No.

                    NAPOLEON
          Fine then! Bye!

Napoleon hangs up the phone.

INT. NAPOLEON'S LIVING ROOM - DAY

Beat. The phone rings as Kip pulls nachos out
of the microwave and sets them on the table.
Kip answers.

                    KIP

          Hello?

                    NAPOLEON
          Kip, just put on your blades and come
          get me!

                    KIP

          Sorry.

                    NAPOLEON
          Well, will you do me a favor then?

                    KIP

          What.

     Beat.

                    NAPOLEON
          Can you bring me my Chap Stick?

                    KIP

          No, Napoleon.

                    NAPOLEON
          But my lips hurt real bad!

                    KIP
          Borrow some from the school nurse.

                    NAPOLEON
          I'm not gonna use hers ya sicko!

                    KIP
          See ya.

Kip hangs up.

INT. HIGH SCHOOL OFFICE - DAY

                    NAPOLEON
          Idiot!

The PRINCIPAL, a balding man in his sixties,
stands with PEDRO, a short and stocky Latino
teenager with a moustache, cowboy boots and
cowboy snap shirt. The Principal points down
the hall.

                    PRINCIPAL
          The cafeteria is at the end of E-hall.

Napoleon approaches them and stops.

                    NAPOLEON
          Hey is that a new kid or something?

                    PRINCIPAL
          Napoleon, this is Pedro. Would you
          mind showin' him where his locker is?

He hands Napoleon a small paper.

                    NAPOLEON
          Sure.

INT. HIGH SCHOOL HALLWAY - DAY

Napoleon tries to open a locker. Pedro stands
next to him; he speaks with a Mexican accent.

                    NAPOLEON
          Yeah there's like a buttload of gangs
          at this school. This one gang kept
          wanting me to join because I'm pretty
          good with a bo-staff.

Napoleon opens the locker. He turns to Pedro.

                    NAPOLEON (CONT'D)
          Do you ride the bus to school?

                    PEDRO
          No, I ride my bike.

                    NAPOLEON
          What kind of bike do you have?

EXT. BIKE RACK - DAY

Napoleon and Pedro stand next to the HIGH
SCHOOL's bike rack. A black mountain bike with
orange handlebars stands between them.

                    PEDRO
          It's a Huffy Sledgehammer.

                    NAPOLEON
          Dang! You got shocks, pegs.

                    PEDRO
          My cousin gave it to me.

                    NAPOLEON
          You ever take it off any sweet jumps?

EXT. PEDRO'S HOUSE - DAY

A jump made from a couple of bricks and
particle board lays on a sidewalk in front of a
small house. Napoleon stands to the side of it.
Pedro rides his bike off the jump. Napoleon
holds his hand a distance from the ground.

                    NAPOLEON
          You got like three feet of air that
          time.

Pedro walks his bike over next to Napoleon.

                    NAPOLEON (CONT'D)
          Can I try it really quick?

                    PEDRO
          Sure.

Napoleon takes the bike and rides it onto the
jump. The board breaks in half and Napoleon
rams the bike into the bricks. Napoleon's
crotch smashes into the cross bar.

                    NAPOLEON
          Owww! Owww! My pack.

INT. NAPOLEON'S KITCHEN - AFTERNOON

An early 1970's style living area. Kip sits at
a computer in the living room. Napoleon stands
behind the counter and drinks a glass of
Kool-Aid. GRANDMA, a butch, round, mulleted
woman wearing chums on her glasses, walks in.
She clears her throat.

                    GRANDMA
          How was school?

                    NAPOLEON
          The worst day of my life, whadya
          think!

                    GRANDMA
          Well, I want you to go and see if
          Tina wants some of this.

She sets a casserole tray on the table.

                    NAPOLEON
          Aaaaaahhhh. Kip hasn't done flippin'
          anything today!

                    GRANDMA
          Look, tonight me and . . .

She notices Kip on the computer not paying
attention.

                    GRANDMA (CONT'D)
          Kip listen!

He turns and faces her.

                    KIP
          What?

                    GRANDMA
          Tonight me and yer Aunt Caroline are
          going to visit some friends and we're
          not gonna be back till tomorrow. We're
          getting' a little low on steak so I've
          got Lyle coming over tomorrow to take
          care of it.

                    NAPOLEON
          Well what's there to eat?!

                    GRANDMA
          Oh, knock it off Napoleon! Make
          yourself a dang quesadilla!

(pronounced kay-sa-dila)

                    NAPOLEON
         Fine!

                    GRANDMA
         I'll be back tomorrow.

Grandma pulls out her keys and leaves. Napoleon
glares at Kip.

                    NAPOLEON
         Stay home and eat all the freakin'
         chips.

                    KIP
         I've been online chatting with babes
         all day. Besides, you know I'm
         training to become a cage fighter.

                    NAPOLEON
         Since when, Kip? You have the worst
         reflexes of all time.

                    KIP
         Try and hit me Napoleon.

                    NAPOLEON
         What?

Kip stands up.

                    KIP
         Try and hit me, come on.

Napoleon stands up. Kip starts poking and
pushing at Napoleon.

                    NAPOLEON
         You're such an idiot.

Napoleon swings at Kip. He blocks it.

The DOOR BELL RINGS. Napoleon relaxes his stance.

                    NAPOLEON (CONT'D)
          I'll get it.

Napoleon quickly slaps Kip in the face.

                         KIP
          Haaaaaaahh!

Napoleon leaves.

EXT. NAPOLEON'S HOUSE - AFTERNOON

DEB, a short plain girl with big hair, wearing
a homemade pink shirt with fake rubies glued to
it, stands at the front door with several
Caboodles, and a flyer in hand.

Napoleon opens the door. Deb looks at her feet.

                         DEB
          Um, hello, would you like to look like
          this?

She hands him a sample glamour shot photo of a
young woman wearing a denim jacket with the
collars flipped up, and frizzed out hair. She
is cross eyed and looking over her shoulder.

                    DEB (CONT'D)
          Because right now for a limited time
          glamour shots by Deb are 75% off.

                    NAPOLEON
          I already get my hair cut at the
          Cuttin' Corral.

                         DEB
          Well, maybe you would be interested in
          some handicrafts.

INT. NAPOLEON'S LIVING ROOM - AFTERNOON

Kip is watching TV. A poorly produced
commercial for "REX-KWON-DO Self Defense" comes
on.

REX, a pasty man with a gut, wearing hammer
pants and amber gradient glasses, stands in
front of a dojo.

> REX
> I'm Rex, founder of the Rex-Kwon-Do
> self defense system. After one week
> training with me in my dojo, you'll be
> prepared to protect yourself with the
> strength of a grizzly . . .

A shot of Rex getting kicked fiercely in the
groin.

> REX (CONT'D)
> . . . the reflexes of a puma . . .

Shot of Rex slapping a gun out of a hand.

> REX (CONT'D)
> . . . and the wisdom of a man.

Shot of Rex putting an older woman in a
headlock.

Rex is standing in front of the dojo again.

> REX (CONT'D)
> Come in today, for your free trial
> lesson.

The address appears. Kip writes it down.

EXT. NAPOLEON'S HOUSE - AFTERNOON

Deb is still showing Napoleon her homemade
crafts.

                              DEB
          And here we have boondoggle key
          chains, a must have for this season's
          fashion.

                           NAPOLEON
          I already made a finity of those at
          scout camp.

Deb looks at the ground.

                              DEB
          Well, is anyone else here? I'm trying
          to earn money for college.

INT. NAPOLEON'S LIVING ROOM - AFTERNOON

Kip is facing the T.V., but turns his head
toward the front door.

                              KIP
          Your mom goes to college!

EXT. NAPOLEON'S HOUSE - AFTERNOON

Deb looks past Napoleon, reacting to Kip. She
begins to shake as if to cry. She looks up at
Napoleon, puts her hand over her mouth and runs
away, leaving her Caboodles behind. Napoleon
stands confused, he closes the door.

EXT. NAPOLEON'S BACKYARD - AFTERNOON

Napoleon stands looking into a fenced yard.

                           NAPOLEON
          Tina you fat lard come get some
          dinner!

A mangy looking LLAMA prances over toward
Napoleon. Napoleon is disgusted but hand feeds
the casserole to it.

EXT. NAPOLEON'S HOUSE - AFTERNOON

Kip sits on the front steps of the house
putting on his Rollerblades. He wears a
sleeveless t-shirt and a pair of sweat pants.
Napoleon approaches him and stops with the
casserole dish in hand. Kip looks up and
notices him as he lashes his blades.

                    KIP
        I need you to pull me into town.

Napoleon scowls.

EXT. NEIGHBORHOOD STREET - AFTERNOON

Napoleon is riding a girl's 10-speed bike, Kip
is on his Rollerblades being pulled with a rope.

INT. REX'S DOJO - AFTERNOON

REX, the same self-defense instructor, wearing
USA hammer pants and amber gradient glasses,
stands in the front of the class. He sounds
like a pro wrestler.

                    REX
        I don't care what they say! If I am
        gonna attack a young pretty woman, a
        little freakin' pepper spray and a kick
        to my groin isn't gonna do anything! My
        name is Rex, and if you sign up for my
        eight week program, you will learn the
        self-defense system I developed after
        fighting for two seasons in the Octagon!
        It's called Rex-Kwon-Do! People may ask
        themselves, what about Judo? What about
        Kung-Fu? Well I'm gonna show you right
        now that those systems don't got jack
        on Rex-Kwon-Do! I need a volunteer.

Napoleon and Kip are standing in the class. Kip
raises his hand.

>   REX (CONT'D)
>   Alright! You, get up here! Bow to your
>   sensei!

Kip stands, walks up to Rex and bows.

>   REX (CONT'D)
>   Now, grab my arm . . . other arm. Now
>   watch. Is what you're gonna do, is
>   break the wrist and walk away! Break
>   the wrist and walk away.

Rex does a bunk move and jerks his arm loose.

>   REX (CONT'D)
>   It's just that simple. Now, try to
>   kick me.

Kip hesitates.

>   REX (CONT'D)
>   Come on, kick me.

Kip kicks softly. Rex blocks it with his shin.

>   REX (CONT'D)
>   Do it again!

Kip kicks, Rex blocks.

>   REX (CONT'D)
>   Do it again!

Kip kicks, Rex blocks.

>   REX (CONT'D)
>   Do it again!

Kip kicks, Rex blocks. Rex turns to the class.

                    REX (CONT'D)
          You'll block it every time! Have a
          seat!

Kip sits down by Napoleon.

                    REX (CONT'D)
          Now, on top of what you just saw, here
          is a small sample of the things you
          will learn if you sign up for my eight
          week program! First off, in Rex-Kwon-
          Do we use the buddy system. No more
          flyin' solo! Whatchoo gonna do when
          you get jumped cuz your wearin' a pair
          of blue British Knights on someone
          else's turf?!

Napoleon raises his eyebrows in agreement.

                    REX (CONT'D)
          You need someone watchin' your back at
          all times, cuz Jiu-jitsu don't work in
          gang-bang! Second off, my pupils will
          learn to discipline their image! Do
          you think I got where I am today
          because I dressed like Peter Pan over
          here?

He points to Napoleon. Napoleon shamefully
turns his head to see if anyone else is looking
at him.

                    REX (CONT'D)
          Hell no! Do you people see what I'm
          wearin'? Do you think someone wants to
          get a roundhouse kick in the face,
          while I'm wearin' these bad boys?

He grabs the sides of his hammer pants.
Napoleon shakes his head in agreement.

                    REX (CONT'D)
        Forget about it! And last off, you'll
        learn to get self-respect! Do you
        think anyone thinks I'm a failure cuz
        I got Starla to go home to at night?

Rex points to a picture of Starla on the wall.
She is a tough body builder/American gladiator-
looking woman with a muscular neck, super tan
skin, and big bleached hair. She also sports a
forced smile.

                    REX (CONT'D)
        Forget about it! Now, for only three
        hundred dollars, I can sign you up
        right now, for my full eight week
        program.

EXT. NEIGHBORHOOD STREET - EVENING

Napoleon rides a girl's 10-speed. Kip is being
tugged with a rope on his Rollerblades.

                    KIP
        Well that place was a rip-off.

EXT. NAPOLEON'S HOUSE - MORNING

Napoleon walks out of his house to wait for the
bus. He wears a t-shirt tucked into a pair of
hammer pants similar to Rex's. He also is
carrying Deb's Caboodles. He stops and looks
across the road.

LYLE a farmer, stands facing a cow in the
field. Napoleon raises his hand to wave.

                    NAPOLEON
        Hey, Lyle.

Lyle slowly waves back. Napoleon looks on. Lyle
pulls a six-shooter-pistol out from his jacket
and points it at the cow. He clicks back the
hammer.

Napoleon looks on. A school bus screeches to a
halt in front of Lyle and the cow, blocking
Napoleon's view. A BANG is heard. Napoleon
flinches.

INT. SCHOOL BUS - MORNING

All the KIDS on the bus scream.

INT. HIGH SCHOOL CLASSROOM - DAY

A finger presses play on a cassette player.
SOFT ROCK MUSIC begins to play.

TWO TEENAGE GIRLS perform sign language in
synchronization to the music. Two OTHER GIRLS
perform sign language to the music also.

Napoleon and a GIRL stand performing sign
language together. He does a two fist splash
which turns into a butterfly that flaps its
wings high above his head.

A classroom of unimpressed STUDENTS sit at
their desks and watch.

Napoleon really gets into it.

Don watches from his desk.

Napoleon does more sign language.

INT. HIGH SCHOOL LOCKER ROOM - DAY

Two moon boots sit on a bench. Napoleon, suited up
in gym clothes, reaches for them and begins to put
them on. Don and TWO JOCKS sit across from him.

                    JOCK
Hey Napoleon, I hear you're in a club
for girls.

                  NAPOLEON
Shut up, I am not!

                    JOCK
Then why are you in the Happy Hands
club?

                  NAPOLEON
Cuz I didn't have a freakin' choice!
All the other sweet clubs were already
filled up! Gosh!

The three boys laugh to themselves and then
leave. Napoleon scowls.

               NAPOLEON (CONT'D)
    Idiots.

He sees Pedro dressed in gym clothes as he
closes his locker.

EXT. HIGH SCHOOL TRACK - DAY

A group of gym students warm up at a track.
Napoleon and Pedro sit on some bleachers. Both
wear gym clothes.

                  NAPOLEON
    So me and you are pretty much friends
    by now, right?

                   PEDRO
    Yes.

                  NAPOLEON
    So you got my back and everything?

> PEDRO

What?

> NAPOLEON

Nevermind.

Beat.

> NAPOLEON (CONT'D)

Have you heard about the dance?

> PEDRO

Yeah.

> NAPOLEON

So, have you met anyone to ask yet?

> PEDRO

No, but I probably will after school.

> NAPOLEON

Who you gonna ask?

Pedro gazes out into the field.

> PEDRO

That girl over there.

He points to SUMMER, a cute blonde who stands
by some friends in the middle of the track. She
puts her hair in a scrunchy.

> NAPOLEON

Summer Wheatley? How the heck are you
gonna do that?

> PEDRO

Build her a cake or something.

                    NAPOLEON
          Yeah, my old girlfriend from Oklahoma
          was gonna fly out here for the dance
          but she couldn't because she's doing
          some modeling right now.

                     PEDRO
          Is she hot?

Napoleon pulls out his Velcro wallet and takes
out the trial glamour shot photo.

                    NAPOLEON
          See for yourself.

Pedro takes the picture. The girl has big hair,
a denim jacket with the collars flipped up, and
is cross-eyed.

                     PEDRO
          Wow.

                    NAPOLEON
          Yeah, I took her to the mall to get
          some glamour shots for her birthday
          one year.

                     PEDRO
          I like her bangs.

                    NAPOLEON
          Me too.

INT. HIGH SCHOOL CAFETERIA - DAY

Pedro and Napoleon eat their hot lunches
silently.

                    NAPOLEON
          How long did it take you to grow that
          moustache?

                    PEDRO
          A couple of days.

                    NAPOLEON
          Wish I could grow one.

Napoleon quickly takes a bite of a Tater Tot
and looks at Pedro's tray of Tater Tots.

                    NAPOLEON (CONT'D)
          You gonna eat your Tots?

                    PEDRO
          No.

                    NAPOLEON
          Can I have 'em?

Pedro nods his head.

                    NAPOLEON (CONT'D)
          Yes!

Napoleon reaches over and grabs them all in one
handful. With the other hand he unzips a zipper
pocket on his pant leg. He quickly glances at
Pedro and then stuffs the Tater Tots into his
leg pocket and zips it up. He looks up and
notices Deb.

She sits down at a nearby table and opens her
sack lunch.

                    NAPOLEON (CONT'D)
          See that girl over there. She came
          over to my house the other night.

Deb takes a bite of her sandwich.

                    PEDRO
          Why?

                    NAPOLEON
        I dunno, but she left all this crap on
        my porch.

                    PEDRO
        She's pretty good looking.

                    NAPOLEON
        Do you dare me to go talk to her?

                    PEDRO
        Sure.

Napoleon walks over and sits across from Deb.
They look at each other. She sips her milk.

                    NAPOLEON
        I see you're drinkin' one percent. Is
        that cuz you think you're fat?

Deb freezes.

                    NAPOLEON (CONT'D)
        Cuz you're not, you could be drinkin'
        whole if you wanted.

Deb looks down at her sandwich.

                    NAPOLEON (CONT'D)
        Well I have all your equipment in my
        locker. You should probably come get
        it cuz I can't fit my nun-chuks in
        there anymore.

A piece of bread and peanut butter is stuck to
her upper lip. Her voice is muffled with bread.

                    DEB
        Where's your locker?

INT. HIGH SCHOOL HALLWAY - DAY

Napoleon and Deb stand at his locker. He yanks
the Caboodles out. She carefully bungees them
to her suitcase roller.

                    NAPOLEON
          Hey can I have one of your key chains?

Deb hands him one and walks off. Napoleon clips
the boondoggle key chain onto his belt loop.
Napoleon watches her leave.

EXT. SAND DUNES - DAY

An ATV speeds across a sand dune. ANGLE ON
Grandma as she rides the ATV full of excitement.

                    GRANDMA
          Woohoo! Woohoo! Woo woo!

She drives past her sister CAROLINE (65) who
sits on the tailgate of a blue truck. TWO
YOUNGER MEN wearing crop-tops and sunglasses
stand next to Caroline. They cheer Grandma on
as she passes.

Grandma continues riding excitedly. She suddenly
hits a bump, catches some air and is thrown
from the ATV. She bounces hard across the sand
and the ATV tips over.

Caroline and the Two Younger Men stare blankly
at the accident.

EXT. AIRSTREAM - DAY

UNCLE RICO (40), with David Hasselhoff-style
hair, glasses, a gold chain, a tight mock
turtleneck shirt, and ankle boots, stands
outside his Airstream throwing footballs at a
video camera on a tripod. The phone RINGS from
inside. He stops and walks inside the Airstream.

INT. HIGH SCHOOL CLASSROOM - DAY

Napoleon sits at his desk reading a book on
Bigfoot. Beat. He slowly lowers the book. His
hand reaches down to his bulging pant leg
pocket. He grabs the zipper and slowly starts
to unzip it. His eyes slowly glance around to
see if anyone notices. He pulls out a Tater
Tot. A couple fall out onto the ground.

Randy with a book in hand, notices.

Napoleon slowly brings one to his mouth and
munches it. The CRUNCH is very audible.

                    RANDY
        Gimme one of your Tater Tots Napoleon!

                    NAPOLEON
        No! Go find your own!

                    RANDY
        Come on gimme some of your Tots!

                    NAPOLEON
        No! I'm freakin' starved. I didn't
        even get to eat anything today!

Randy scowls at him and kicks Napoleon's Tot-
pocket from across the aisle. His pocket oozes
with grease and potato. Napoleon glares at
Randy.

INT. NAPOLEON'S KITCHEN - DAY

A note on the fridge reads: NAPOLEON, DON'T
FORGET TO FEED TINA. LOVE GRANDMA. Napoleon
stands staring at it.

                    NAPOLEON
        Gosh!

EXT. NAPOLEON'S BACKYARD - AFTERNOON

Napoleon walks out of a sliding glass door. He holds a casserole dish and walks towards the fence.

                    NAPOLEON
          Tina! Come and eat some ham!

Napoleon stops and watches a car approach from down the dirt road.

EXT. NAPOLEON'S HOUSE - AFTERNOON

A tattered Buick stops in front of the house, loud NEW AGE MUSIC is blasting. Uncle Rico steps out and stretches.

Napoleon walks over to him. Uncle Rico speaks with a back country/semi-southern accent.

                    NAPOLEON
          What are you doing here Uncle Rico?

                    UNCLE RICO
          Grandma took a little spill at the
          sand dunes today, broke her coccyx.

(Pronounced cock-ix)

                    NAPOLEON
          What! Since when does she go to the
          dunes?

                    UNCLE RICO
          Looks like there's a lot you don't
          know about.

Uncle Rico pulls a brief case out of the car and walks past Napoleon toward the house. Napoleon stands motionless holding the casserole.

INT. NAPOLEON'S KITCHEN - AFTERNOON

A greasy piece of steak being cut with a knife
and a fork. Uncle Rico is standing behind the
counter, he raises a piece of meat to his mouth
and beings to chew it. He washes it down with a
large, glass mug of whole milk.

Napoleon and Kip are sitting at the kitchen
table quietly watching Uncle Rico. Uncle Rico
chews on more steak. BEAT.

                    KIP
          So when's Grandma coming back?

                    UNCLE RICO
          Not sure.

                    NAPOLEON
          You don't have to stay with us. We're
          not babies.

                    UNCLE RICO
          Talk to your Aunt Caroline.

Uncle Rico takes a sip of milk.

                    NAPOLEON
          Well Kip is like thirty-two years old!

                    KIP
          I don't mind if you stay.

                    UNCLE RICO
          Thanks Kip.

Kip nods back at Uncle Rico. Napoleon notices.

                    NAPOLEON
          Gosh! What the flip was grandma doing
          at the sand dunes?

                    UNCLE RICO
          She was on a date with her boyfriend.

                    NAPOLEON
          Her boyfriend?

                    UNCLE RICO
          You guys wanna see my video?

                    KIP
          I do.

Kip gets up and leaves to the living room.

                    NAPOLEON
          Gracious!

INT. NAPOLEON'S LIVING ROOM - AFTERNOON

A VHS tape is shoved into a VCR. Uncle Rico
sits down in a chair next to Napoleon and Kip
who are on a couch. Uncle Rico holds a remote
and hits play.

The TV screen shows Uncle Rico throwing some
footballs at the camera that's filming him.

Napoleon, Kip and Uncle Rico watch intently.

The TV screen shows Uncle Rico pick up the
balls under the camera, sprint back to his
first position and start throwing again.

                    UNCLE RICO
          Whadya think?

                    KIP
          It's pretty cool I guess.

Napoleon glares at Kip.

                    UNCLE RICO
          Wish I could go back in time. I'd take
          state.

Uncle Rico watches the screen.

                    NAPOLEON
          This is pretty much the worst video
          ever made.

                    KIP
          Like anyone can know that one.

                    UNCLE RICO
          You can leave Napoleon!

                    NAPOLEON
          You guys are retarded!

Napoleon gets up and leaves.

INT. BURGER JOINT - EVENING

Uncle Rico and Kip sit at a booth eating milk
shakes.

                    KIP
          Napoleon's been getting on my nerves
          lately.

Uncle Rico spoons some shake into his mouth.

                    KIP (CONT'D)
          Are you and Tammy still together?

Uncle Rico looks away.

                    UNCLE RICO
          Not really.

Beat.

                         KIP
          Why is that?

                     UNCLE RICO
          She got jealous. Said I was still
          livin' in '82. How about your
          girlfriend?

                         KIP
          Well, its getting a little bit serious
          right now. We talk online for at least
          two hours a day. But it's going pretty
          good. Right now I'm trying to raise
          some money so I can fly her out for a
          couple of days.

Kip spoons some shake into his mouth.

                     UNCLE RICO
          What does she look like?

                         KIP
          She's blonde. Has a pretty good
          looking face. But I'm getting kind of
          T.O.ed cuz I haven't seen a full body
          shot yet.

                     UNCLE RICO
          Well I've got a little project I can
          pay you for.

Takes a drink of some shake.

                         KIP
          Really? That sounds good.

EXT. SUMMER'S HOUSE - AFTERNOON

A big nice house. Pedro and Napoleon lay on
their stomachs peering through some vegetation.

                         NAPOLEON
          Go for it.

Pedro stands up. Holding a cake he runs across
the street to the house. Napoleon looks on.

Pedro steps up to the porch and slowly sets the
cake down in front of the door. He rings the
doorbell and then runs. Napoleon waits on his
bike, Pedro stands on the pegs and they ride off.

EXT. NAPOLEON'S HOUSE - AFTERNOON

Kip and Uncle Rico sit on the front steps. Each
are holding a paper plate with a couple of
steaks on them.

                       UNCLE RICO
          Back in '82 I used to be able to throw
          a pig skin a quarter mile.

                           KIP
          Are you serious?

                       UNCLE RICO
          I'm dead serious.

Napoleon and Pedro ride up on the bike.

                   UNCLE RICO (CONT'D)
          Watch this.

Uncle Rico grabs Kip's uneaten steak and hurls
it at Napoleon and Pedro. It hits Napoleon in
the hair.

                         NAPOLEON
          What the heck are you doing!

Uncle Rico throws his arms up in the air as if
to say 'bring it on.'

                              PEDRO
          I better go.

Pedro rides off quickly.

Napoleon rubs his hair and walks away.

                              KIP
          That's what I'm talking about.

Uncle Rico sits back down next to Kip.

                          UNCLE RICO
          How much you wanna bet I can throw a
          football over them mountains? If coach
          woulda put me in fourth quarter we
          woulda been state champions. No doubt.
          No doubt in my mind. You better
          believe things would be different now.
          Woulda gone pro in a heartbeat. I'd be
          makin' millions. Livin' in a mansion
          somewhere. Soakin' it up in a hot tub
          with my soul mate.

Beat. Uncle Rico looks over at Kip.

                     UNCLE RICO (CONT'D)
          Kip, I reckon you're pretty good in
          cyberspace. Ever come across anything
          like . . . time travel?

                              KIP
          Easy. I've already looked into it for
          myself.

                          UNCLE RICO
          Right on.

EXT. HIGH SCHOOL BASKETBALL COURT - DAY

Napoleon stands by a tether-ball ball pole. He holds the rope and looks around the area for Pedro. People play basket ball and some girls jump rope. Napoleon takes a step back and throws the tether-ball. It swings back around and he punches it repeatedly.

He stops, grabs the rope and looks around again. Summer holds a jump rope and talks with friends. She looks at Napoleon. Napoleon smiles. He takes a step back and throws the ball as hard as he can. It swings back around and Napoleon jumps and hits it with his knee.

Napoleon stops and looks to see if Summer was watching. Summer smiles at Napoleon. She mouths something to her friends, puts down her jump rope, and runs over to Napoleon. Napoleon grins.

                    SUMMER
        Is Pedro here today?

                    NAPOLEON
        I don't think so. Why?

                    SUMMER
        Just wondering. Can you give this to
        him for me?

She hands Napoleon a note. She turns to leave.

                    NAPOLEON
        Hey Summer.

She turns back around.

                    NAPOLEON (CONT'D)
        Wanna play me?

Napoleon holds up the tether-ball. Summer shakes her head slowly and then runs back to her friends. Napoleon watches. He opens the note. It reads: "NO".

INT. HIGH SCHOOL HALLWAY - DAY

It's passing period. Napoleon stands alone by his locker. He is wearing the same hammer pants again but a different t-shirt. He looks around for Pedro.

Randy walks by and shoves Napoleon into a locker. Randy leaves. Napoleon does a delayed kick to the air in Randy's direction.

INT. HIGH SCHOOL CAFETERIA - DAY

Napoleon eats a bowl of chili by himself. Deb sees him from another table.

EXT. HIGH SCHOOL STEPS - DAY

Napoleon sits on some steps in front of the high school. He draws a picture of a liger. Deb walks out of the school and stands behind him.

                    DEB
          What are you drawing?

                  NAPOLEON
          A liger.

Napoleon signs his name and writes the date. Deb sits down on the steps, three feet from him.

                    DEB
          What's a liger?

                  NAPOLEON
          It's pretty much my favorite animal.
          It's like a lion and a tiger mixed,
          bred for its skills in magic.

                         DEB
           Huh. Where's your friend?

                       NAPOLEON
           I dunno. Did you see him today?

                         DEB
           No.

                       NAPOLEON
           Neither did I.

                         DEB
           Do you need a ride?

                       NAPOLEON
           No, I missed the bus but my uncle is
           coming to get me.

                         DEB
           Oh.

Uncle Rico pulls over next to the curb and
honks. NEW AGE MUSIC blares from the car radio.
Napoleon looks up.

                       NAPOLEON
           See yah.

Napoleon quickly gets up, runs to the car and
gets in. Deb looks on.

INT. NAPOLEON'S HOUSE - DAY

Napoleon grabs the telephone off the wall. It
has a 50 foot phone cord attached to it. He
stops, looks at Kip and Uncle Rico, walks out
of the kitchen, around a corner, through the
hall and into his backyard. Stretching the
phone cord the whole way.

EXT. NAPOLEON'S BACKYARD - DAY

Napoleon closes the door, dials a number, then
puts the phone to his ear.

INT. PEDRO'S HOUSE - DAY

A phone RINGS. Pedro's sister CORRINA answers
the phone.

CORRINA

> Bueno?

NAPOLEON

> Hello?

CORRINA

> Who's this?

NAPOLEON

> Napoleon Dynamite.

CORRINA

> Who?

NAPOLEON

> Napoleon Dynamite. I'm one of Pedro's
> best friends.

CORRINA

> Your last name is Dynamite?

NAPOLEON

> Yeah. Is Pedro there?

CORRINA

> What kinda name is that? No, he's not
> here right now.

NAPOLEON (QUICKLY)

> 'Kay bye.

Napoleon quickly presses the receiver.

INT. NAPOLEON'S KITCHEN - DAY

Napoleon walks into the kitchen with the phone.
He stops.

Uncle Rico and Kip are sitting at the kitchen
table. Uncle Rico is holding a pen above a note
pad. They both turn and glare at Napoleon.
Beat.

                    NAPOLEON
          What?

Uncle Rico turns to Kip.

                    UNCLE RICO
          Why don't we take this somewhere a
          little more private.

                    KIP
          Good idea.

Napoleon looks at them. Uncle Rico and Kip
stand up and leave.

INT. BOWLING ALLEY - DAY

A bowling ball bounces off the bumper-bowling
rails as it makes its way to the pins. A large
amount of pins get knocked down.

Kip stands at the head of the lane. Uncle Rico
can be seen sitting down behind him at the
score table.

                    KIP
          Yes!

Kip takes a seat next to Uncle Rico.

                    UNCLE RICO
Before we get started on our little
project I have a few concerns. First off
I'm a little concerned about your
transportation situation. I mean, do you
got a car you can borrow from someone?

                    KIP
Well, that's the problem right now. At
the moment nothing comes to mind.

Uncle Rico sighs.

                    UNCLE RICO
You can borrow my car for the time
being. I do better on foot anyway.
Okay. We also need to find a way to
make us look official. Like we have
all the answers.

                    KIP
How about some gold bracelets?

BEAT.

                    UNCLE RICO
We need like some name-tags. With our
pictures on 'em. All laminated and
what not. I mean we gotta look legit.

                    KIP
That's true.

                    UNCLE RICO
Is there some place around here that
we can get our picture taken? Like
some kind of studio or somethin'?

BEAT.

INT. DEB'S STUDIO - AFTERNOON

Deb stands in her studio with a camera. A rack
of denim jackets and colorful prom gowns is
behind her.

                    DEB
          Turn your head on more of a slant.

Uncle Rico sits on a bar stool. He wears a
denim jacket with the collars flipped up. A
pink backdrop with stars is draped behind him.
Uncle Rico turns his head.

                    DEB (CONT'D)
          Perfect. Okay, now make a fist and
          slowly ease it underneath your chin.

Uncle Rico makes a fist and slowly places it
underneath his chin.

                    DEB (CONT'D)
          This is looking really good.

                    KIP
          You can say that again.

                    DEB
          Okay, hold still. Just imagine that
          you're weightless. You're in the ocean
          and you're surrounded by little sea
          horses.

Uncle Rico softly squints his eyes and cracks a
slight smile. Deb snaps a picture.

                    DEB (CONT'D)
          That was the one. That's gonna come
          out really nice.

Uncle Rico relaxes.

UNCLE RICO
Yeah that felt pretty good, I'm really
relaxed. Thanks Deb. Your up Kip.

KIP
Is there some kind of vest I can wear?

INT. HIGH SCHOOL CAFETERIA - DAY

Pedro sits at a table eating lunch by himself.
BEAT. Napoleon walks in and sits down next to
him with his lunch.

NAPOLEON
Where have you been?

PEDRO
I got sick.

NAPOLEON
How come?

PEDRO
Two days ago I went to my cousins
birthday party . . .

EXT. PARK - DAY

Pedro stands looking at a picnic table full of
Mexican food. He holds a paper plate under his
mouth as he chomps on a taco full of carne
asada.

PEDRO
. . . and they had all this food so I
started to eat this taco with lots of
meat.

Pedro darts his eyes around and wrinkles his
brow.

                    PEDRO (CONT'D)
          It was like a carne asada taco, and all
          the sudden I started to feel really
          evil inside, and kind of sad you know.

INT. PEDRO'S BATHROOM - DAY

Pedro lays in a bubble bath. Motionless. He
blinks twice.

                    PEDRO
          So the next day I just like laid in
          the bath tub for a couple of
          hours . . .

INT. HOSPITAL WAITING ROOM - DAY

Pedro sits in a lobby next to TWO OLDER MEXICAN
WOMEN.

                    PEDRO
          . . . and then I had to go the
          hospital because my aunt was having a
          baby.

Pedro pulls a bag of chips out from a vending
machine.

                    PEDRO (CONT'D)
          We had to wait a really long time in
          the lobby so I bought a little bag of
          corn tortillas from the vending
          machine . . .

Pedro eats some chips. He stops, looks at his
body, and then curiously examines a chip.

                    PEDRO (CONT'D)
          . . . and right when I started eating
          them I felt really good inside. The
          weird feeling I was having just like
          lifted out of me. It like evaporated
          into nothing.

INT. HIGH SCHOOL CAFETERIA - DAY

Pedro hold his milk.

                    PEDRO
          So, I don't know. I think they was
          like some holy chips or something.

Napoleon stares at Pedro, his mouth slightly
open and a napkin stuffed in the neck of his
shirt.

                    NAPOLEON
          Has Summer said anything to you yet?

                    PEDRO
          No. Not yet.

                    NAPOLEON
          Well, she said no.

                    PEDRO
          She did?

Pedro looks at his food.

                    PEDRO (CONT'D)
          Well what about that other girl?

                    NAPOLEON
          What other girl?

                    PEDRO
          The one that left all the crap on your
          porch.

                    NAPOLEON
          You mean Deb?

                    PEDRO
          Yeah her.

                    NAPOLEON
          What about her?

                     PEDRO
          Well I asked her out too.

                    NAPOLEON
          What?

Pedro notices Deb approaching, looks down at
his food. Napoleon looks over his shoulder to
see if he can see Deb.

Deb approaches the table with her sack lunch
and note in hand. Napoleon turns back around
and starts eating.

Pedro shoves food around with a spoon. His
other hand rests on the table. Deb's hand
slides into frame and puts a note underneath
his hand. Pedro's eyes dart over at the note
and then up at Deb. She winks at him and then
leaves.

Napoleon glares at Pedro.

INT. HIGH SCHOOL HALLWAY - DAY

Pedro unfold's the note. It reads: "Yes." Pedro
and Napoleon hover over the note, they stand in
front of some lockers. Pedro folds the note
back up and puts it in his pocket.

                    NAPOLEON
          Well nobody's gonna go out with me!

                     PEDRO
          Have you asked anybody yet?

                    NAPOLEON
          No! But who would? I don't even have
          any good skills.

                        PEDRO
          What do you mean?

                        NAPOLEON
          You know, like nun-chucks, bow-
          hunting, computer hacking. Girls only
          want boyfriends that have great
          skills!

                        PEDRO
          Aren't you pretty good at drawing like
          animals and warriors and stuff?

                        NAPOLEON
          Yes. Probably the best that I know of.

                        PEDRO
          Just draw a picture of the girl you
          wanna take out and then give it to her
          for like a gift or something.

                        NAPOLEON
          That's a pretty good idea.

INT. NAPOLEON'S HOUSE - DAY

A yearbook full of student pictures. Napoleon
puts his finger under the name Trisha Stevens,
and then moves his finger across the page until
he arrives at her photo.

Napoleon smiles. He has a white piece of paper
and a pencil. He beings to draw her face.

INT. COUPLE'S LIVING ROOM - DAY

Uncle Rico sits at a table with LANCE and
SHONEY, a young couple. Uncle Rico wears a
short sleeve shirt, tie and name-tag with his
glamour shot on it. An array of Tupperware
rests on the table.

                    UNCLE RICO
          Now if you guys decide to invest in
          the twenty-four piece set, I'm gonna
          throw in a gift.

                    LANCE
          Well, what's the gift?

Uncle Rico raises his eyebrows, reaches under
the table and pulls out a decorative mini-sail
boat. He sets it on the table.

                    UNCLE RICO
          Bet you folks don't have one of these
          now do yah?

SHONEY looks at Lance.

                    SHONEY
          I want that.

                    UNCLE RICO
          'Kay then. Now, this ain't yer run-a-
          the-mill crapperware guys, these are
          some serious Nupont fiber woven bowls.

                    LANCE
          So, if we buy the 24 piece set, the
          mini-sailboat is included?

                    UNCLE RICO
          That is correct, sir. Now, my buddies
          down at NASA use these same Nupont
          micro-fibers to make helmets and
          special tiles for the space shuttle.
          'Kay?

Uncle Rico looks at Lance.

                    UNCLE RICO (CONT'D)
          Lance, you look like a strong young
          pup.

Uncle Rico hands him a bowl.

                    UNCLE RICO (CONT'D)
              Try and tear this bowl.

Lance tries to rip it in half. Uncle Rico and
Shoney watch. He gives up and hands it back.

                    UNCLE RICO (CONT'D)
              You guys see what I mean?

INT. COPY STORE - DAY

Napoleon stands at the cashier counter. A WORKER
wearing an apron stands on the other side.

                    NAPOLEON
              Can you guys laminate this for me?

Napoleon hands him his picture of Trisha. The
worker looks at it. We don't see the picture yet.

EXT. NEIGHBORHOOD STREET - DAY

A Tupperware bowl is shoved under a car tire.
Kip walks around the car and gets in. A LATINA
WOMAN stands on her lawn watching him.

Kip turns on the car and backs up over the
bowl. The woman watches intently. The smashed
bowl resumes its original form. Kip opens the
door and stands up out of the car.

                    KIP
              Pretty cool.

EXT. TRISHA'S HOUSE - DAY

A nice house. Napoleon walks up to the door
with a paper bag in hand.

Napoleon knocks on the door.

INT. TRISHA'S LIVING ROOM - DAY

KNOCK at the door. Uncle Rico and ILENE,
Trisha's mother sit on opposing couches. Ilene
wears stretch pants and a matching top that are
bejeweled and puff painted. She is obnoxiously
happy and never stops smiling. Tupperware-style
products lay on the floor. Ilene gets up.

                    ILENE
          Excuse me.

She opens the front door. Napoleon stands
looking at her.

                    NAPOLEON
          Hi, is uh, Trisha here?

                    ILENE
          You know, she's not. She's at a
          friends house right now.

                    UNCLE RICO
          Hey Napoleon!

Napoleon looks past Ilene. Uncle Rico waves at
him. Napoleon's face goes blank.

                    UNCLE RICO (CONT'D)
          Napoleon's my nephew.

Ilene looks back to Napoleon.

                    ILENE
          That's nice! Well, one thing's for
          sure, you two sure are handsome!

Ilene smiles. Uncle Rico shrugs and grins to
himself.

                    NAPOLEON
          Yeah, um, could you give this to her
          for me.

Napoleon hands Ilene the bag.

                    ILENE
          I certainly could, good lookin'!

                    NAPOLEON
          Thanks.

Napoleon turns and leaves.

                    ILENE
          Uh-huh! Good-bye!

She closes the door. Ilene sits back down
across from Uncle Rico.

                    UNCLE RICO
          Poor kid. I've been taken care of him
          while his grandma's in the hospital.
          He wets the bed and everything.

                    ILENE
          You're kidding! That breaks my heart!

                    UNCLE RICO
          Oh yeah. He's a tender little guy.
          Changed his last name to Dynamite in
          Junior High. Still gets beat up and
          what not. Anyhow, are we still feeling
          pretty good about this thirty-two
          piece set?

INT. NAPOLEON'S KITCHEN - AFTERNOON

Napoleon holds Kip in a tight headlock. They
struggle.

                    NAPOLEON
          What the crap was Uncle Rico doing at
          my girlfriends house?!!!

                                              49

                              KIP
              Let go Napoleon! You're bruising my
              neck meat.

Napoleon lets go. Kip straightens out and rubs
his neck.

                           NAPOLEON
              What the heck are you guys doing!
              Trying to ruin my life? Make me look
              like a friggin' idiot?

                              KIP
              I'm out making some moola with Uncle
              Rico.

Kip rubs his hand on his neck and then looks at
his hand.

                         KIP (CONT'D)
              I think you ripped my mole off.

                           NAPOLEON
              I did?

                              KIP
              Yeah. Is my neck bleeding?

Napoleon looks at the back of his neck.

                           NAPOLEON
              A little bit.

Kip glares at Napoleon. Beat. Uncle Rico walks
in.

                          UNCLE RICO
              Hey Kip.

Napoleon glances angrily at Uncle Rico.

                    UNCLE RICO (CONT'D)
          I wish you wouldn't look at me like
          that Napoleon.

                    NAPOLEON
          I wish that you'd get out of my life
          and shut-up!

Uncle Rico stands still and stares at Napoleon.
Beat.

                    UNCLE RICO
          While your out playing patty-cake with
          Peddrow, Uncle Rico's out makin'
          himself a hundred and twenty bucks.

                    NAPOLEON
          I can make that much money in five
          seconds!

                    KIP
          Yeah right Napoleon. I made seventy-
          five bucks today.

                    NAPOLEON
          Bull, Kip. You're on welfare.

                    KIP
          I can still make a few bucks on the
          side.

                    UNCLE RICO
          Well Napoleon. Looks like you don't
          have a job. So why don't you go feed
          Tina.

                    NAPOLEON
          Why don't you go eat a decroded piece
          of crap?

INT. TRISHA'S LIVING ROOM - EVENING

Trisha stands holding the paper bag. She reaches inside and pulls out Napoleon's laminated picture. She first reads a handwritten note on the back of it. It reads: "THERE'S A LOT MORE WHERE THIS CAME FROM. IF YOU GO TO THE DANCE WITH ME. YOURS TRULY, NAPOLEON DYNAMITE"

                    NAPOLEON
          There's a lot more where this came
          from. If you go to the dance with me.
          Yours truly, Napoleon Dynamite.

Trisha turns the sheet over to see the picture.

Beat.

Trisha appears frightened.

                    ILENE
          You know you're gonna go with that boy
          to the dance.

Trisha turns and sees her mother standing by the couch. She Drops the picture of a hideous sketch portrait that looks more like a Sasquatch than a girl. The eyes are spaced very far apart from each other. The mouth is small and the nose narrow. "TRISHA" is written in cursive at the bottom of the portrait.

EXT. CHICKEN FARM - DAY

A FARMER wearing overalls addresses Napoleon and THREE YOUNGER KIDS outside of an enormous chicken barn. Lyle stands next to the farmer.

                         FARMER
          By noon I need them eight-thousand
          hens moved into their new cages.
          Sometimes they don't wanna cooperate,
          but just give 'em a good shake and
          they should settle down for ya.

Napoleon raises his hand.

                        NAPOLEON
          Do they have large talons?

                         FARMER
          Do they have what?

                        NAPOLEON
          Large talons?

                         FARMER
          Boy, I don't understand a word you
          just said.

Napoleon shifts his stance a bit and shrugs.

                      FARMER (CONT'D)
          Okay, meet me back out here at noon
          and we'll have a little lunch waiting
          for you.

INT. CHICKEN BARN - DAY

Napoleon struggles to take a chicken out of its
cage. He pulls it out and it flaps its wings
wildly. He can't seem to get it under control.
Finally he shakes it and it goes limp. He
stuffs it in the new cage.

The Three Younger Kids try to move the
ferocious chickens into their new cages.

Napoleon struggles with two more chickens and
puts them in their cages.

EXT. CHICKEN FARM - DAY

A picnic table with a bowl of hard boiled eggs, egg salad sandwiches and orange juice. The Farmer stands over the pitcher of orange juice with an egg in his hand. He cracks the egg and then empties its contents into the pitcher of juice. The BUZZ of flies can be heard.

Napoleon and the kids look on.

Farmer begins to mix the juice and egg with a large spoon.

>   FARMER
>   Well, dig in.

Napoleon walks over to the table and grabs a sandwich. The kids follow his lead. Napoleon takes a bite of his sandwich. A kid bites into a hard boiled egg. Another kid bites into an egg sandwich. Lyle chews a hard boiled egg. A different kid takes a bite of his sandwich. With dry yoke and egg in his mouth, Lyle points off in the distance and begins to say something. Muffled with egg and old age, he is entirely inaudible.

>   FARMER (CONT'D)
>   Down in the creek bed I found some
>   Shoshone Indian arrowheads.

Napoleon takes a bite of a hard boiled egg as he struggles to understand. The Farmer takes a sip of orange juice. The other kids try to listen. Napoleon drinks some orange juice. Beat. His gag reflex kicks in slightly.

>   FARMER (CONT'D)
>   Can't find my checkbook, so I hope you
>   don't mind if I pay you in change.

INT. NAPOLEON'S KITCHEN - DAY

Napoleon sits at the table counting piles of
change. Pedro sits across from him. Napoleon
thinks for a moment.

                    NAPOLEON
          Six dollars. That's like a dollar an
          hour.

The phone rings. Napoleon answers.

                    NAPOLEON (CONT'D)
          Hello.

INT. TRISHA'S LIVING ROOM - DAY

Trisha sits on a couch with a phone to her ear.
Her mother sits next to her.

(Intercut with Napoleon in kitchen)

                    TRISHA
          Is Napoleon there?

                    NAPOLEON
          Yeah.

                    TRISHA
          Can I talk to him?

                    NAPOLEON
          You already are.

                    TRISHA
          Oh. Napoleon, this is Trisha. I'm just
          calling to tell you that I can go to
          the dance with you. And I also wanted
          to thank you for the beautiful drawing
          you did of me. It's hanging in my
          bedroom.

Ilene nods her head. Trisha rolls her eyes.

                    NAPOLEON
          Really? It took me about three hours
          to do all the shading on your upper
          lip. It's probably about the best
          drawing I've ever done.

                    TRISHA
          It's really nice.

                    NAPOLEON
          Yeah, well I'll probably just pick you
          up at six for the dance. Is that okay?

                    TRISHA
          That's fine.

                    NAPOLEON
          'Kay. Bye.

                    TRISHA
          Bye.

INT. NAPOLEON'S KITCHEN - DAY

Napoleon hangs up the phone and sits down.

                    PEDRO
          Who was that?

                    NAPOLEON
          Trisha.

                    PEDRO
          Who's she?

                    NAPOLEON
          My woman that I'm taking to the dance.

                    PEDRO
          Did you give her a drawing?

                    NAPOLEON
          Heck yes I did.

                     PEDRO
          Well what are you going to wear to the
          dance?

                    NAPOLEON
          Just like a silk shirt or something.
          What are you wearing?

                     PEDRO
          Deb has something for me. But you
          should probably get a suit.

Napoleon and Pedro look at each other from
across the table.

INT. THRIFT STORE - DAY

A mannequin sports a three-piece brown 70s style
suit. Soft LOUNGE MUSIC plays in the background.

Napoleon and Pedro study the suit.

                    NAPOLEON
          Pedro, how do you feel about that one?

                     PEDRO
          Looks nice.

                    NAPOLEON
          It looks sweet. Awesome.

Pedro walks up to the mannequin and looks at
the price tag.

                     PEDRO
          It's twelve dollars.

                    NAPOLEON
          Twelve dollars, for that?

                    PEDRO
          Hold on.

Pedro walks over to the woman at the front
register.

                    NAPOLEON
          Gosh! Freakin' rip off.

                    PEDRO
          Do you guys have a layaway program?

                    THRIFT STORE CLERK
          We sure don't.

                    PEDRO
          Okay.

Pedro walks back to Napoleon.

                    PEDRO (CONT'D)
          They don't do layaway.

                    NAPOLEON
          You dare me to just hide it, then I'll
          just come back and buy it later?

                    PEDRO
          That's a good idea.

                                        CUT TO:

Napoleon stands buy a book case and pulls out a
lusty romance book. He walks to the corner of
the store where a security camera is mounted to
the ceiling. Napoleon stands underneath the
camera and looks over to Pedro who is next to
the mannequin.

With his fingers Napoleon signals one, two and
three. Then Napoleon slowly raises the book
cover in front of the camera lens.

INT. SECURITY ROOM - DAY

RENAE, a middle-aged woman, sits at a chair in front of a security monitor. The book cover fills the whole screen. It shows a Fabio like man with his shirt off dipping a busty woman with flowing hair.

Renae appears a little excited.

                    RENAE
          Oooooh.

She slowly stands up with the speed of a snail and begins the trek for the door.

INT. THRIFT STORE - DAY

Napoleon holds the book in front of the camera. Pedro stuffs the suit into an old suitcase.

Renae inches her way down some stairs.

Pedro puts the suitcase back. Napoleon places the book back on the shelf.

EXT. THRIFT STORE - DAY

Napoleon and Pedro exit the thrift store.

INT. THRIFT STORE - DAY

Renae stands in the store, out of breath.

EXT. LA TIENDA GAS STATION - DAY

Pedro sits on a bench in front of the gas station.

INT. LA TIENDA GAS STATION - DAY

Napoleon walks up to the counter.

                    NAPOLEON
          Hey, how's it going?

The CASHIER looks at him.

                    NAPOLEON (CONT'D)
          Those egg rolls are looking pretty
          nice. I'm get me some later,
          but . . . You know what, I think I'll
          just buy me one of them lotto tickets.

The cashier glares at Napoleon suspiciously.

                    NAPOLEON (CONT'D)
          The wife says I gotta quit, but I'm
          just feelin' really positive and . . .

                    GAS STATION CASHIER
          Go home. I'm not selling lottery to a
          minor!

Napoleon leaves, and bumps his knee into a
cooler. He keeps walking.

EXT. LA TIENDA GAS STATION - DAY

Napoleon walks out of the gas station. Pedro
sits on a bench.

                    NAPOLEON
          They wouldn't sell me one. I don't
          look old enough. Dang!

Beat.
                    PEDRO
          Do you think I look old enough?

Napoleon turns his head toward Pedro.

INT. LA TIENDA GAS STATION - DAY

Pedro stands nervously in front of the CASHIER.

                    PEDRO
          Un lotto ticket por favor.

The cashier looks at him suspiciously and then
he looks at Pedro's moustache. ECU of
moustache. The cashier relaxes and then hands
him a lotto ticket.

                    PEDRO (CONT'D)
          Thanks.

EXT. LA TIENDA GAS STATION - DAY

Napoleon waits at the bench in front of the gas
station. Pedro walks out and joins him.

                    NAPOLEON
          Did you get it?

Pedro hands the lotto ticket to Napoleon.

                    NAPOLEON (CONT'D)
          Yes!

Napoleon scratches it with his fingernail.

                    NAPOLEON (CONT'D)
          Yes! Yes! Pedro you picked a great
          one! We won ten bucks!

EXT. MAIN STREET - DAY

In SLOW-MOTION, Napoleon walks down the street
in the brown three-piece suit. He holds a
corsage in his hand.

Napoleon Dynamite

FLIPPIN' SWEET!

INT. NAPOLEON'S KITCHEN - DAY

Uncle Rico holds a slab of steak in his hand
and takes a bite of it, then he sips on a mug
of milk with ice. Napoleon stands on the other
side of the counter.

                    NAPOLEON
          I need you to give me a ride in an
          hour.

                    UNCLE RICO
          Where to?

                    NAPOLEON
          The dance.

                    UNCLE RICO
          Hmm. You takin' my client's daughter?

                    NAPOLEON
          Yes. I gotta pick her up too.

                    UNCLE RICO
          Well Uncle Rico's got a sale to
          finalize up in Banida in five minutes.

                    NAPOLEON
          Can't you just take me and then drop
          me off when you're done or whatever?

Uncle Rico looks at Napoleon and then pours a
big piece of ice into his mouth.

EXT. DIRT ROAD - AFTERNOON

Uncle Rico drives his Buick down a dirt road.
Napoleon sits next to him and the corsage sits
on the dash board.

EXT. FARM HOUSE - AFTERNOON

Napoleon sits in the parked car, Uncle Rico starts to get out.

                    UNCLE RICO
          I'll be back in a minute. Don't
          disturb me while I'm in there.

                    NAPOLEON
          Well hurry up cuz I gotta get Trisha!

Uncle Rico slams the door close and then heads for the house. He knocks on the door and an OLD LADY lets him in.

Napoleon sits in the car all bored. He takes the corsage off the dash, opens the clear plastic box and then smells it. He closes it and puts it back on the dash.

Napoleon looks at the house. Beat. Napoleon looks at his watch. It reads: 5:40 p.m.

Napoleon takes the corsage off the dash and gets out of the car. He jogs up to the house and knocks on the door. Beat. He knocks again. No answer.

He runs back toward the car and then stops. He scans the long and deserted road in front of him. He starts running down the road.

EXT. DEB'S HOUSE - AFTERNOON

A finger touches a door bell. Pedro stands at the door holding a corsage. He wears a blazer with a tee-shirt underneath and some stone-washed jeans. Pedro's AUNT waits behind him in an Astro mini-van.

Deb opens the door. She's dressed in a big pink dress with huge puffy shoulder sleeves. Pedro hands her the corsage. She smiles and walks out. Pedro smiles back.

EXT. DIRT ROAD - AFTERNOON

Napoleon slowly jogs down the empty road. He stops and bends over to catch his breath. He looks at his watch. It reads: 5:55 p.m. Napoleon throws his head back.

                    NAPOLEON
          Gosh!

Napoleon slowly brings his head back down. Beat. HIP HOP BEATS can be heard in the distance. Napoleon notices. He turns his head in the direction of the music.

A slick, low-rider Impala drives down the road with a big cloud of dust trailing behind.

Napoleon watches the car approach. The Impala slows down and stops right in front of him.

CHOLO #1 and CHOLO #2 with shaved heads, white t-shirts, mustaches, and soul patches, sit in the car. Both wear big black sunglasses. They look at Napoleon.

INT. LOW RIDER - AFTERNOON

Napoleon sits in the back of the low rider as it drives down the road.

                    NAPOLEON
          So are you guys Pedro's cousins with
          all the sweet hook ups?

                    CHOLO #1
          True that.

Napoleon nods his head and looks out the window.

EXT. TRISHA'S HOUSE - AFTERNOON

A finger touches the doorbell. Napoleon stands on the porch holding the corsage. The low-rider can be seen behind him in the driveway.

The front door opens to reveal Trisha's dad SHELDON. He studies Napoleon for a moment. Beat.

                    NAPOLEON
          Is Trisha here?

Sheldon notices the low-rider over Napoleon's shoulder. It's front hydraulics bounce the car a bit. HIP HOP BEATS can be heard from the car.

                    SHELDON
          Who's that in my driveway?

                    NAPOLEON
          That's my ride.

                    SHELDON
          Whoa, whoa there big guy! My
          daughter's not going anywhere with you
          and your amigos.

                    ILENE
          Sheldon come here!

Sheldon hesitates and then moves behind the door. He and Ilene can be heard bickering behind the partially closed door. Napoleon shifts a bit and stretches his neck out.

Sheldon opens the door again. Defeated.

                    SHELDON
          Yeah, just make sure she sits by an
          air bag.

                    NAPOLEON
            'Kay.

INT. LOW RIDER - AFTERNOON

Cholo #1 drives, Trisha sits shotgun, and
Napoleon and Cholo #2 sit in the back. They
drive down the street listening to HIP HOP
MUSIC.

INT. HIGH SCHOOL DANCE - EVENING

Teenage couples slowly sway to a SLOW SONG. The
camera ZOOMS through the crowd of bodies to
catch Napoleon and Trisha walking in. They come
in and sit on some chairs next to a wall.

From his seat, Napoleon looks for Pedro.
Different couples bear-hug dance. The camera
ZOOMS in on Pedro and Deb who dance on the
other side of the crowd. They chat happily.

Napoleon tries to get Pedro's attention by
waving his arm. No luck. Napoleon turns to
Trisha, who has her arms folded and is looking
away.

                    NAPOLEON
          You wanna go over there by my friend
          Pedro and dance really quick?

Trisha acts like she doesn't hear. She stands
up quickly and walks over to a group of her
friends sitting on some other chairs. They chat
happily.

Napoleon watches her. He then tries to distract
himself by looking at the dance again.

INT. HIGH SCHOOL BATHROOM - EVENING

Napoleon walks into the bathroom and viciously
pumps the lever on the paper towel dispenser.
He rips off a sheet of brown paper and blows
his nose.

INT. HIGH SCHOOL DANCE - EVENING

Don is among Trisha's friends. He motions his
head towards the exit a few times. Trisha looks
back to where Napoleon was sitting. The chair
is empty. She turns back to her friends and
nods. Trisha and the group leave.

INT. HIGH SCHOOL BATHROOM - EVENING

Napoleon looks at himself in the mirror. Beat.
He takes out a pack of Big League Chew grape
bubble gum. He pulls out a handful, puts it in
his mouth and begins chewing. He exits.

INT. HIGH SCHOOL DANCE - EVENING

Napoleon walks into the dance and looks around.
He stands alone looking for Trisha. Beat.

                    PEDRO
          Napoleon.

Pedro and Deb are standing next to him now.

                    PEDRO (CONT'D)
          When did you get here?

                    NAPOLEON
          A minute ago. Have you guys seen
          Trisha anywhere?

                    DEB
          No.

                    NAPOLEON
          Huh. She probably just went to the
          bathroom. Are you guys having a killer
          time?

                       DEB
          Yes.

Beat. They all watch the dance.

                      PEDRO
          If you can't find her, I'll let you
          dance with Deb for a few songs.

                                        CUT TO:

Napoleon and Deb dance together during a slow
song. They move slowly and awkwardly. Napoleon
raises his hand and tenderly lifts one of her
poufy sleeves at her shoulder.

                    NAPOLEON
          I like your sleeves. They're real big.

                       DEB
          Thanks.

                    NAPOLEON
          So, are you and Pedro getting really
          serious now?

                       DEB
          No. We're just friends.

                    NAPOLEON
          Huh. How's your glamour shots going
          lately?

                       DEB
          Pretty good.

Beat.

                    DEB (CONT'D)
     I could do you a personal portrait
     sometime, if you wanted to come over.

                    NAPOLEON
     Okay.

She looks away and they keep on dancing.

INT. HIGH SCHOOL HALLWAY - EVENING

Pedro takes a drink from the drinking fountain.
He looks up at the wall above the fountain. A
poster reads: CLASS ELECTIONS! TO RUN FOR
PRESIDENT, SIGN UP AT OFFICE.

Pedro studies the sign.

INT. HIGH SCHOOL DANCE - EVENING

Pedro, Napoleon and Deb sit on some chairs.

                    PEDRO
     How do you run for president?

INT. HIGH SCHOOL OFFICE - DAY

An office with a secretary. Pedro and Napoleon
walk up to the desk.

                    NAPOLEON
     Hey, how are you guys doing?

                    SECRETARY
     What can I do for you?

                    NAPOLEON
     How do you sign up to become the
     school president?

                    SECRETARY
     You mean run for office?

                                              69

                    NAPOLEON
          Yes, that's what I mean.

                    SECRETARY
          You need to fill out an application
          and turn it in before three.

                    NAPOLEON
          Where do we get one of those?

                    SECRETARY
          Right there.

She points to a stack of blue papers on a
counter.

                    NAPOLEON
          Thanks.

Pedro grabs an application. As he grabs one,
Summer Wheatley walks up behind him and grabs
one also. She pauses and glares at Pedro for a
second. Then she quickly turns and walks away.

EXT. HIGH SCHOOL STEPS - DAY

Napoleon and Pedro sit on some steps in front
of the school. Pedro reads the blue
application.

                    PEDRO
          Tomorrow I can start putting campaign
          flyers on people's lockers.

Pedro lowers the application and thinks for a
moment.

                    PEDRO (CONT'D)
          What should I put on them?

                    NAPOLEON

I don't know. I could draw like a
really sweet picture of you flying
around on a dragon. Then we could have
it say "Reach For The Stars".

                     PEDRO

What about the FFA competition?

                    NAPOLEON

Oh yeah. When is it?

                     PEDRO

Tomorrow.

                    NAPOLEON

Crap.

Beat.

                     PEDRO

Do you think people will vote for me?

                    NAPOLEON

Heck yes. I'd vote for you.

                     PEDRO

Like, what are my skills?

                    NAPOLEON

Well, you got a sweet bike, you're
pretty good at hooking up with chicks.
Plus you're like the only guy at
school that has a moustache.

                     PEDRO

That's true.

                    NAPOLEON

If you need to use any of my skills
I'll do whatever you want.

                    PEDRO
     Thanks.

Beat.

                 PEDRO (CONT'D)
     If I win, you can be my secretary or
     something.

                   NAPOLEON
     Sweet! Plus I could be your bodyguard
     too, or like a secret service captain
     or whatever.

                    PEDRO
     Okay.

INT. NAPOLEON'S HOUSE - DAY

A homemade time machine sits on the kitchen
table. It is a gray metal box with a knob on
it, a counter to punch in the date, a wire
going from the box to a metal headband, and a
metal headband that has a wire going to a metal
T-handle with a ball on the end.

A white piece of paper is taped to the box. It
reads: Don't Touch!.

Napoleon stands looking at it. He glances over
at Kip who is typing on the computer.

                   NAPOLEON
     Is that yours?

                     KIP
     Don't touch it. It's Uncle Rico's.

                   NAPOLEON
     What's it for?

Napoleon sits down at the table to examine it
further.

                    KIP
          It's a time machine. He bought it
          online.

                    NAPOLEON
          Yeah right.

                    KIP
          It works Napoleon. You don't know.

                    NAPOLEON
          Have you guys tried it yet?

                    KIP
          No.

Napoleon grabs a photocopied packet entitled:
"Time Machine Modulus: User's manual".

                                        CUT TO:

Napoleon has the metal head band strapped to
his head. He looks over to the wall. The time
machine is plugged into a socket. Napoleon
looks at the manual. It shows a clip-art man
holding the T-handle between his legs.

Napoleon does the same. Kip watches as he walks
in place nervously.

                    KIP (CONT'D)
          Don't do it Napoleon.

Napoleon darts his eyes over at his brother and
then back at the box on the table.

He looks at the on/off switch.

                    NAPOLEON
          Dare me?

                    KIP
          Napoleon, don't.

Napoleon takes a deep breath. Beat. He reaches over and flips on the switch. A red light above the switch comes on and a low HUM can be heard.

Napoleon feels a sudden surge of pain in his groin and head. He jerks around in his seat.

                    NAPOLEON
        Oww! Owww! Oww! It hurts! Turn it off!

Kip runs over and unplugs it. Napoleon grunts in pain. Kip watches curiously.

                    NAPOLEON (CONT'D)
        I forgot to put in the crystals.

Kip grabs a Ziploc bag of crystals on the counter.

                    NAPOLEON (CONT'D)
            Put 'em in the crystal holder right
            there.

Napoleon points to a small metal cup mounted to the top of the box. Kip puts them in.

                    KIP
        Are you ready?

                    NAPOLEON
        Yeah hold on.

Napoleon repositions the T-handle between his legs.

                    NAPOLEON (CONT'D)
        'Kay. Turn it on.

Kip plugs in the time machine. A low HUM is heard instantly.

Napoleon squints is eyes to endure the pain. A
CRACKLING noise can be heard. BEAT. Napoleon
starts to twitch a bit.

                    NAPOLEON (CONT'D)
          Oww! Oww! My pack! Turn it off!

Uncle Rico stands in the hallway watching. He
holds a briefcase.

Kip unplugs it. Napoleon closes his eyes and
turns his head up to the ceiling in pain.

                    NAPOLEON (CONT'D)
          It's a piece of crap. It doesn't work.

                    UNCLE RICO
          I could'a told you that.

Napoleon and Kip turn and see Uncle Rico.
SILENCE.

INT. GROCERY STORE - AFTERNOON

Uncle Rico pushes a grocery cart down an aisle.
He walks as if he's favoring his groin.
Napoleon walks into frame, also favoring his
groin, and puts a pack of markers in the cart.
Uncle Rico looks at them.

                    UNCLE RICO
          I said the sixteen pack not the
          thirty-eight! You're just gonna hafta
          mix and match! Now put 'em back!

                    NAPOLEON
          Gosh.

Napoleon grabs the markers and walks out of
frame. Uncle Rico keeps pushing the cart.

Summer Wheatley is the cashier. She punches some numbers into the cash register. She glances at Napoleon and Uncle Rico who load groceries onto a conveyer belt. Uncle Rico notices a box of individualized chips.

> UNCLE RICO
> Napoleon, you know we can't afford the fun packs! We're not made of money! Take 'em back and get some Pampers for you and your brother.

Napoleon looks at Summer angrily. She grins. Napoleon leaves.

INT. FFA AGRICULTURE BUILDING - DAY

A jar of milk is brought up to Napoleon's lips. He takes a drink. He sets it back down on the table where there are other jars of milk with numbers on them. A banner hanging from the table reads: Future Farmers of America. THREE FFA JUDGES with clipboards and blue corduroy jackets stand behind him.

Napoleon move his tongue around in his mouth.

> NAPOLEON
> The defect in that one is bleach.

Beat.

> JUDGE #1
> Correct.

> NAPOLEON
> Yes!

Napoleon brings another jar of milk to his mouth and drinks. He sets the jar back down.

                    NAPOLEON (CONT'D)
          It tastes like this cow got into an
          onion patch.

Judge #1 raises his eyebrows and nods to JUDGE
#2.

                    JUDGE #1
          Correct.

                    NAPOLEON
          Yes!

INT. FFA BARN - DAY

A set of cow utters. Pedro is kneeling down
studying them. An OLD JUDGE stands behind him
with a clipboard.

                    PEDRO
          They are pretty good except for one
          little problem.

Pedro points his finger at a fifth nipple on
the udder.

                    PEDRO (CONT'D)
          That little guy right there. He is
          nipple number five. A good dairy cow
          should only have like four.

                    OLD JUDGE
          Well done.

INT. FFA AGRICULTURE BUILDING - DAY

Napoleon takes a sip of another jar of milk. He
sets it back on the table. He thinks. Beat.

                    NAPOLEON
          Delicious. It's fine. It's just good
          old fashioned whole milk.

The judges compare their clipboards. Beat.

                    JUDGE #1
          Correct again, you're in first place.

                    NAPOLEON
          Yes! Yes!

Napoleon makes a fist.

INT. HIGH SCHOOL HALLWAY - DAY

A series of shots of buttons being placed onto
shirts. The buttons read: SUMMER FOR PRESIDENT.

Summer, Trisha, Don and others pass them out to
kids during passing period. Lockers are adorned
with flyers of Summer's face and text that
reads: Vote for Summer.

Pedro and Napoleon stand in the hall, with gold
medals around their neck, watching them pass
out the campaign buttons.

Pedro wipes some sweat off of his forehead with
his index finger.

                    PEDRO
          Do you think its kind of warm in here?

                    NAPOLEON
          No.

                    PEDRO
          I think they have the heater on or
          something.

                    NAPOLEON
          Its seems pretty good to me.

                    PEDRO
          You don't feel like your head is
          burning or anything?

                    NAPOLEON
     No.

                     PEDRO
     I'm gonna go home and lay down.

                    NAPOLEON
     'Kay. See yah.

Pedro turns and leaves.

Napoleon takes a bite of a roll. Don approaches
him with a button.

                      DON
     Vote for Summer.

He tries to hand Napoleon a button.

                    NAPOLEON
     Yeah right. I'm not voting for her.

                      DON
     Who are you gonna vote for Napoleon?

                    NAPOLEON
     I'm voting for Pedro Sanchez! Who do
     you think?

Don starts laughing. He shakes his head and
starts to leave.

                 NAPOLEON (CONT'D)
     Hey, can I still have one of those
     buttons?

Don looks at him warily and then hands him one.
Napoleon grabs it, quickly turns, and violently
hurls it down the other end of the hall.

The hall immediately goes SILENT as Summer,
Trisha and others look on. Napoleon immediately
runs down some stairs to his right.

INT. BURGER JOINT - DAY

Uncle Rico and Kip sit across from each other
eating onion rings and shakes.

                    KIP
          That guy in Florida give you your
          money back yet?

                    UNCLE RICO
          I sent him an email sayin' I was gonna
          notify the authorities if I didn't get a
          refund in full . . . But don't you ever
          wish that you could go back? I mean with
          all the knowledge you have now?

                    KIP
          I guess so.

                    UNCLE RICO
          I tell you what, you'd find your soul-
          mate . . .

                    KIP
          I've already got a soul-mate.

                    UNCLE RICO
          What was her name again?

                    KIP
          LaFawnduh.

                    UNCLE RICO
          Yeah, LaFawnda. How's she doin'?

                    KIP
          I think I'm gonna need some time off,
          she's coming out from Detroit for a
          few days.

                    UNCLE RICO
          Well what about work? Have you studied
          up on the new product?

                         KIP
          Yes.

                    UNCLE RICO
          Do you know it back to front?

                         KIP
          Basically.

                    UNCLE RICO
          Well try to sell some to that
          girlfriend of yours.

Kip looks squarely at Uncle Rico.

                         KIP
          She doesn't need it.

Uncle Rico chews an onion ring.

EXT. PEDRO'S HOUSE - DAY

Pedro sits on his driveway with his bike upside
down. He wears a hooded sweatshirt with the
drawstrings pulling the hood tight around his
face. He works on the bike.

Napoleon approaches from the sidewalk. He holds
a Trapper Keeper.

                    NAPOLEON
          Hey. I did some drawings for the
          flyers.

Pedro turns the pedals on his bike around.

                    PEDRO
          Thanks.

                    NAPOLEON
        Why do you got your hood on like that?

                     PEDRO
        Well, when I came home from
        school . . .

INT. PEDRO'S KITCHEN - DAY

Pedro stands in his kitchen and drinks a tall
glass of ice water.

                     PEDRO
        . . . my head started to get really
        hot, so I drank some cold water, but
        it didn't do anything.

INT. PEDRO'S BATHROM - DAY

Pedro lays in a bubble bath.

                     PEDRO
        So I laid in the bath tub for a while,
        but then I realized that it was my hair
        that was making my head so hot . . .

INT. PEDRO'S KITCHEN - DAY

Pedro stands in his kitchen with an electric
razor and starts shaving his head.

                     PEDRO
        . . . so I went in my kitchen and
        shaved it all off.

EXT. PEDRO'S HOUSE - DAY

Pedro sits next to his bike.

                     PEDRO
        I don't want anyone to see.

Napoleon stares at him.

INT. DEB'S STUDIO - AFTERNOON

Napoleon and Deb stand behind a table of
mannequin heads with wigs on them. Pedro is
sitting down on a stool. Deb hands Napoleon a
curly red wig. Napoleon grabs at it but grabs
Deb's hand instead.

                    NAPOLEON
          Sorry.

Deb looks away shyly. She grabs another wig off
a mannequin head. It's brown and manly.

                    DEB
          This one matches your season Pedro.

                    PEDRO
          Thank you.

EXT. HIGH SCHOOL - MORNING

A bewigged Pedro and Napoleon pull up to the
high school on the Huffy. Napoleon stands on
the pegs. They get off the bike and go in.

INT. HIGH SCHOOL HALLWAY - MORNING

An empty quiet hallway. Another empty quiet
hallway. Pedro and Napoleon stand and enjoy the
silence.

SNAP ZOOMS. A roll of tape, Pedro rips a piece
off. Napoleon slams a flyer on a locker, over
the top of a Summer flyer. It reads: REACH FOR
THE STARS WITH PEDRO. It shows a sketch of
Pedro flying on a dragon with stars above him.

Pedro rips off a piece of tape. Napoleon slams
a flyer on a wall of tile, above a drinking
fountain, on a door, on a vending machine,
above some urinals, etc.

Napoleon and Pedro walk over to a locker and look at it. It's covered with Summer campaign paraphernalia.

A blue school bell RINGS.

EXT. HIGH SCHOOL STEPS - MORNING

A boondoggle key-chain is placed into a hand. Another boondoggle key-chain is placed into a different hand.

                    NAPOLEON
          Vote for Pedro. Vote for Pedro.

Napoleon and Pedro stand in front of the school doors passing out key-chains to arriving students. Napoleon wears a T-Shirt with iron-on letters that read: VOTE FOR PEDRO. Pedro wears a vaquero blazer with a white shirt and bolo-tie and a brown wig with a part in it.

                    PEDRO
          Reach for the stars with Pedro.

Pedro hands a key-chain to a girl.

                    NAPOLEON
          Vote for Pedro.

Napoleon hands a key chain to a student.

Summer and Trisha stand by a tree and watch.

A key-chain is attached to a belt loop, another is placed on a finger like a big ring, and one is attached to an FFA jacket zipper and then zipped up.

INT. HIGH SCHOOL HALLWAY - DAY

Nathan, a small teenager with braces, puts some
books into his locker. Randy walks up behind
him and pinches his neck with his hand. Nathan
shrinks in pain.

                    RANDY
          Nathan. Let me borrow fifty cents so I
          can get a pop.

                    NATHAN
          I don't have any Randy.

                    RANDY
          Come on Hessidy, I'll pay you back.

                    NATHAN
          Don't!

                    RANDY
          Hessidy!

Napoleon sips from a drinking fountain and
notices the scuffle.

Randy pinches Nathan's neck harder. Nathan
begins to bend over in pain.

                    NATHAN
          Stop! Stop! Here.

Nathan pulls some change out of his pocket and
hands it to Randy. Randy leaves. Nathan rubs
his neck.

                    NAPOLEON
          Hey . . .

Nathan turns and sees Napoleon standing next to
him.

                    NAPOLEON (CONT'D)
              How's your neck doing?

                         NATHAN
              Stings.

                         NAPOLEON
              That's too bad.

Napoleon pulls a boondoggle key chain out of
his jacket and hands it to Nathan.

                    NAPOLEON (CONT'D)
              Pedro offers you his protection.

Nathan looks down at the key chain in his hand
and then back up at Napoleon.

EXT. BIKE RACK - DAY

The combination on a cheap bike lock is
unlocked. Nathan pulls his bike off the bike
rack. Randy approaches him.

                         RANDY
              Nathan. Let me borrow your bike. I'll
              give you two king size nut-rolls and
              some chips when I bring it back.

                         NATHAN
              No.

Nathan tries to leave but Randy grabs the
handle bars and they fight over the bike.

HIP-HOP BEATS can be heard. Cholo #1 and #2
pull up to the curb in their low-rider. A sign
written in Gothic calligraphy is mounted to the
side of their car. It reads: Vote 4 Pedro.

Randy stops and looks at the car. Cholo #1 shakes his head at Randy who lets go of the bike and runs off.

Nathan glances over at the car, Cholo #1 gives him a casual nod.

INT. HIGH SCHOOL HALLWAY - DAY

A group of NERDY BOYS put out their hands. Pedro gives each one a boondoggle key chain.

EXT. BUS STATION - DAY

Kip waits at a bus station holding a cardboard sign that reads: LaFawnduh. A vase of flowers is at his feet.

People file out of a big charter bus. Kip looks for LaFawnduh.

A pair of gold high-heels step down from the bus. The camera tilts up to reveal LAFAWNDUH, a tall, sexy, busty, black woman with long blonde hair.

Kip smiles. At ground level we see Kip's shoes and the vase of flowers. The pair of gold heels rush into frame and accidentally kick over the vase of flowers, as the two embrace.

EXT. NEIGHBORHOOD STREET - AFTERNOON

Trisha and Summer walk down the sidewalk slowly. Uncle Rico's car slowly creeps up alongside them. He sticks his head out the window and stops the car next to them.

                    UNCLE RICO
          Hey, are you Trisha?

                    TRISHA
          Yeah.

                    UNCLE RICO
        Do you remember me? I'm one of your
        mom's friends. I'm Napoleon's uncle?

Trisha glances at Summer.

                    TRISHA
        Oh, yeah.

                    UNCLE RICO
        Could you do me a favor and give a
        couple of these to your mom for me?

Uncle Rico hands Trisha a handful of peach
colored flyers.

                    UNCLE RICO (CONT'D)
        Just tell her she can pass them out to
        her friends or whoever.

                    TRISHA
        Okay.

                    UNCLE RICO
        Now you gals feel free to give me a
        call if you could use some.

Uncle Rico grins at them, and then drives off.

Trisha looks at the flyer. It reads: BUST PLUS!
INCREASE YOUR BREAST SIZE IN DAYS! THE NATURAL
WAY. A picture of a busty lady in a sweater.

INT. HIGH SCHOOL CLASSROOM - DAY

Napoleon sits at his desk. Randy sits next to
him.

                    RANDY
        Hey, Napoleon. I hear your family
        sells breast enhancer for a living.

                    NAPOLEON
          Bull! Where'd you hear that?

                     RANDY
          Her.

Randy points to Trisha who sits at the front of
the class. Napoleon scowls.

INT. HIGH SCHOOL HALLWAY - DAY

Napoleon walks down the hall during passing
period. Napoleon's locker is covered in peach
BUST PLUS flyers.

He stares at it.

EXT. PARK - DAY

Kip and Lafawnduh sit at a picnic table. Kip
spoons a glob of milk shake. He slowly reaches
across the table and puts it into Lafawnduh's
mouth.

She closes her eyes and swallows it in
pleasure.

Beat. Kip watches her. She looks back at him
and studies his eyes. She slowly reaches for
his face, hesitates, and then lifts off his
glasses. She sets them on the table.

She pulls out a black velvet jewelry box and
sets it on the table. She opens it up. Kip
looks inside. Lafawnduh pulls out a thick gold
chain. Kip raises his eyebrows. She reaches
over and puts it on him.

EXT. NEIGHBORHOOD STREET - AFTERNOON

Uncle Rico drives down the street. A grapefruit
hits the driver's side door. Uncle Rico slams
on the brakes and looks out the window.

Napoleon stands at the side of the road by a tree. He looks at Uncle Rico and then makes a run for it. Uncle Rico gets out of the car and bolts after him.

They run across a small field. Napoleon slips on some leaves and falls. Uncle Rico jumps on top of him and puts him in a headlock. They struggle on the ground.

> UNCLE RICO
> Why in the hell you throwin' crap at my Buick, Napoleon?

> NAPOLEON
> Everyone at school thinks I'm a freakin' idiot cuz of you!

Uncle Rico tightens his hold and they roll on the ground. Napoleon grunts in pain.

> UNCLE RICO
> You gonna clean my car now? Huh?

> NAPOLEON
> Let go of me, you bodagget!

Napoleon lands a chop to his kidneys. Uncle Rico lets go. Napoleon storms off.

EXT. HIGH SCHOOL - DAY

Pedro and Deb stand in front of the high school. Pedro looks at his watch.

> PEDRO
> Napoleon is supposed to be here. Have you seen him?

> DEB
> No.

                         PEDRO
          That's weird.

Pedro reveals that he's holding onto a rope. He
gives it a few tugs.

The rope is attached to a pinata effigy of
Summer that is hanging from a tree. It bobs up
and down as a blind-folded BOY swings at it with
a broom-handle. Other TEENAGERS cheer him on.

EXT. THRIFT STORE - DAY

Napoleon walks down the street and goes into
the thrift store.

INT. THRIFT STORE - DAY

Napoleon tries on a fanny pack and then puts it
back on the rack.

He handles a pair of nun-chuks.

He looks through a pile of video tapes. He
pulls one out. It reads: D-QWON's DANCE
GROOVES. The cover shows a smiling black man
wearing a head microphone. A 50 cent price
sticker is on the cover also. Napoleon's eyes
grow big.

                                      CUT TO:

Napoleon drops two quarters into the CASHIER'S
hand.

EXT. THRIFT STORE - DAY

Napoleon walks quickly out of the store.

INT. HIGH SCHOOL OFFICE - DAY

Pedro sits on a chair outside of the
principal's office. Deb looks at him from the
hallway. The PRINCIPAL opens the door.

                    PRINCIPAL
          Peddrow, step into my office please.

Pedro looks up at the Principal and goes
inside.

INT. PRINCIPAL'S OFFICE - DAY

The principal sits at his desk. Pedro looks at
him blankly.

                    PRINCIPAL
          Look Peddrow, I don't know how they do
          things down in Juarez, but here in
          Idaho we have a little something
          called pride. Understand? Smashing in
          the face of a pinata that resembles
          Summer Wheatley is a disgrace to you,
          me and the entire gem state!

INT. NAPOLEON'S BEDROOM - DAY

Napoleon sits on his bed scratching his head.
He blankly looks around the room. Beat.

Napoleon pulls the D-Qwon's Dance Grooves video
out of his jacket and looks at it.

He hits the eject button on his VCR and the
cassette holder pops up. He inserts the tape
and hits play.

Napoleon closes the door to his room. From
outside the closed door we hear a happy MUSIC
INTRO and then D-Qwon's voice.

                    D-QWON
          Hi, I'm D-Qwon! Are you ready to get
          your groove on?

                    NAPOLEON
          Yes.

                    D-QWON
          Okay, let's get started!

INT. HIGH SCHOOL HALLWAY - DAY

Pedro stands in an empty hallway taking his
flyers off lockers and crumpling them up.

EXT. HIGH SCHOOL STEPS - DAY

Pedro sits on some steps thinking. Deb comes
down and sits next to him.

                    DEB
          Are you disqualified?

                    PEDRO
          No. They just made me take down all my
          flyers as a penalty for the pinata.

                    DEB
          Can you still run for President?

                    PEDRO
          Yeah. I don't understand, he said
          you're not allowed to smash pinatas
          that look like real people. But we do
          it in Mexico all the time.

Beat.

                    DEB
          Your hair looked great today.

                    PEDRO.
          Thank you.

                    DEB
          I can make some more boondoggle if you
          ran out.

                    PEDRO
          That's okay. I still have a lot.

                    DEB
          Alright. See you tomorrow Pedro.

Pedro waves good-bye, Deb leaves.

INT. NAPOLEON'S KITCHEN - AFTERNOON

Napoleon stands in front of the fridge with his
back to us. He pours himself a glass of red
Kool-Aid. He turns around, his face is sweaty
and his shirt has sweat stains on it. DANCE
MUSIC can be heard coming from his room.
Napoleon takes a drink.

Lafawnduh sits at the kitchen table looking at
Napoleon. Napoleon notices her and chokes on
his drink. Beat. She speaks with a low and sexy
voice.

                    NAPOLEON
          Who are you?

                    LAFAWNDUH
          I'm LaFawnduh.

                    NAPOLEON
          What are you doing here?

                    LAFAWNDUH
          I'm waiting for Kip.

                    NAPOLEON
          Kip?

                    LAFAWNDUH
          Why are you so sweaty?

                    NAPOLEON
          I've been practicing.

                    LAFAWNDUH
          Practicing what?

                    NAPOLEON
          Some dance moves.

Napoleon quickly takes a gulp of Kool-Aid.

                    LAFAWNDUH
          You like dancing.

The sound of a DOOR CLOSING. Kip comes in. He
looks entirely different. No glasses, sports a
gold chain, a ribbed turtle neck sweater, a
poufy vest and baggy jeans.

                    KIP
          Well my chores are done.

Napoleon stares at Kip, shocked.

                    KIP (CONT'D)
          Are you ready Lafawnduh?

                    LAFAWNDUH
          I am honey.

                    KIP
          Sorry Napoleon, we're running a little
          late for some prime rib. Tell Uncle
          Rico not to wait up for me.

LaFawnduh pulls a cassette tape out of her
purse.

                    LAFAWNDUH
          You might like this, my cousin made
          it.

LaFawnduh hands the tape to Napoleon.

                    LAFAWNDUH (CONT'D)
          I'll be outside waitin' baby. Bye
          Napoleon.

LaFawnduh leaves.

                    NAPOLEON
          See ya.

Kip watches her leave. Kip sighs.

                    KIP
          LaFawnduh's been the best thing that's
          happened to me. I'm hundred percent
          positive she's my soul mate . . . I'm
          sure there's a babe out there for you
          too somewhere.

Beat. They awkwardly look at each other.

                    KIP (CONT'D)
          Peace out.

Kip leaves.

                    NAPOLEON
          See ya.

EXT. HIGH SCHOOL BASEBALL FIELD - DAY

A gym class plays kickball. Napoleon is on the
mound, he rolls the ball to a BOY at the plate.
The boy kicks the ball over Napoleon and runs
to first base.

Summer comes up to the plate. Napoleon holds the ball. Don and Trisha stand behind the fence.

                    DON
          Come on Summer! Home run!

Summer gives Napoleon a crusty look. Napoleon looks at Pedro who is playing short stop. Napoleon looks back at Summer and rolls the ball.

Summer bunts it with her foot and sprints towards first base. Napoleon scrambles for the ball and then launches it as hard as he can at Summer. It hits her leg with a SLAP and makes her trip and fall on the ground.

                    SUMMER
          Aaaah!

Napoleon pants like a wolf. Trisha and Don run over to help Summer.

                    DON
          Oh, yeah. You're a big man Napoleon.
          Real tough.

Napoleon walks to the bench. The teams change sides. Summer gets up and limps to her position in right field. Pedro steps up to the plate. Don takes his position with the ball on the mound.

                    DON (CONT'D)
          You're gonna lose tomorrow. You know
          it Pedro.

Pedro rubs his moustache. Don rolls the ball, Pedro drills it out into the field. He runs to first base. Safe.

Napoleon steps up to the plate.

                    DON (CONT'D)
Hey Napoleon, you wet the bed last
night?

                    NAPOLEON
Hey Don, did you take a dump in your
bed last night?

                    DON
I could kick your butt Napoleon. So
I'd shut up.

                    NAPOLEON
Why don't you go tell your mom to shut
up!

                    DON
What did you say?

                    NAPOLEON
Whatever I feel like I wanna say!

                    DON
Did you just say something about my
mom?

                    NAPOLEON
Maybe I did, maybe I didn't!

                    DON
You wanna die Napoleon?

                    NAPOLEON
Yeah right. Who's the only one here
that knows illegal ninja moves from
the government?

Don steps right up to Napoleon's face.

                    DON
Step up.

They exchange looks. SILENCE. Pedro watches
from first base. Summer and Trisha watch from
the outfield.

Napoleon quickly slaps Don in the face. SLAP!
Don squeals like a girl.

                    DON (CONT'D)
          Haaaaaah!

Don bends over and holds his face. Napoleon
runs off the field as fast as he can. Pedro
looks down at the ground.

EXT. DIRT ROAD - DAY

Napoleon runs down a dirt road next to some
power lines.

INT. HIGH SCHOOL HALLWAY - DAY

Pedro stares blankly at a poster on the wall.
It reads: Election Assembly tomorrow! Candidate
Speeches Etc.

EXT. JOHNSON RESERVOIR - DAY

Napoleon stands at the edge of a lake with a
fishing pole and viciously casts out his line.
It makes a PLOP sound as it hits the water.

EXT. PEDRO'S HOUSE - DAY

Pedro rides his bike up to his house, puts the
kick stand up and goes inside. The bike falls
as he walks away from it.

EXT. JOHNSON RESERVOIR - DAY

Napoleon reels in a small fish. He grabs the
line and takes the fish off the hook.

INT. PEDRO'S KITCHEN - DAY

Pedro sits at his table writing on a piece of
paper.

EXT. JOHNSON RESERVOIR - DAY

Napoleon drop kicks the fish back into the
water.

INT. PEDRO'S BATHROOM - DAY

Pedro lays in a bubble bath. He submerges his
head.

INT. DEB'S STUDIO - DAY

Uncle Rico stands by a rack of prom gowns, he
fondles one of their necklines.

Deb is pulling down a backdrop of a library
scene.

                    DEB
        Is this what you're looking for?

                  UNCLE RICO
        Well, I was thinking something a
        little more soft around the edges.

He continues to smooth out the bodice of a prom
gown with his fingers.

                    DEB
        Well I have a nice soft pink sheet
        that I could hang and then I could
        wrap you in foam or something billowy.

                  UNCLE RICO
        Billowy is good.

Uncle Rico walks towards Deb. He stands very close to her. She is oblivious to his sudden closeness and goes on jabbering.

                    DEB
          It would be really nice if I got the
          fan going and hung some tinsel from
          the top.

Deb turns to find Uncle Rico intimidatingly close.

                    UNCLE RICO
          You know Deborah you have striking
          features, such a soft face should be
          complimented with a soft body.

Deb drops the pink sheet.

                    DEB
          Mr. Rico . . .

                    UNCLE RICO
          My friends and clients call me Uncle
          Rico.

                    DEB
          What are you-

                    UNCLE RICO
          Don't say another word, Napoleon told
          me you'd be interested.

                    DEB
          Napoleon?

Uncle Rico quickly unbuttons the vest he is wearing.

Deb gasps.

Uncle Rico takes out a Bust Plus Pamphlet from his shirt pocket. He sets it on a stool.

                    UNCLE RICO
          Call me when you're ready.

Uncle Rico winks at her and then saunters out.

Deb stands frozen. She looks at the pamphlet on the stool.

INT. NAPOLEON'S HOUSE - DAY

The phone RINGS.

Napoleon's bedroom door is mostly closed but through a crack we see him following along to D-Qwon's Dance Grooves. The phone RINGS LOUDLY.

INT. NAPOLEON'S KITCHEN - DAY

Napoleon, sweating profusely, grabs the phone.

                    NAPOLEON
          Hello?

EXT. PHONE BOOTH - DAY

Deb stands at a rural phone booth with phone in hand.

(Intercut with Napoleon in kitchen)

                    DEB
          Napoleon?

                    NAPOLEON
          Yeah. Who's this?

                    DEB
          It's Deb. And I'm calling to let you
          know that I think you're a shallow
          friend.

                    NAPOLEON
          I don't even know what you're talking
          about.

                    DEB
          Don't lie Napoleon. Your Uncle Rico made
          it very clear how you feel about me.

                    NAPOLEON
          What?!

                    DEB
          I don't need herbal enhancers to feel
          good about myself, and if you're so
          concerned about that, why don't you
          try eating some yourself?

Napoleon listens with a blank look on his face.
BEAT.

                    DEB (CONT'D)
          Also, Pedro told me that you slapped
          Don in the face today. I hope that
          doesn't disqualify him from giving his
          speech tomorrow.

Deb hangs up on Napoleon.

INT. NAPOLEON'S KITCHEN - DAY

Napoleon slowly pulls the phone away from his
ear and hangs it up.

EXT. NAPOLEON'S BACKYARD - DAY

Uncle Rico stands throwing footballs toward a
camera on a tripod. Napoleon walks out the
back-door of the house.

                    NAPOLEON
          Grandma just called and said you're
          supposed to go home now.

Uncle Rico stops and looks at Napoleon. Beat.

                    UNCLE RICO
          She didn't tell me anything.

He throws a football.

                    NAPOLEON
          Too bad. She said she doesn't want you
          here when she gets back because you've
          been ruining everybody's lives and
          eating all our steak.

                    UNCLE RICO
          I'm not going anywhere Napoleon.

                    NAPOLEON
          Get off my property!

                    UNCLE RICO
          It's a free country. I can do what I
          want.

                    NAPOLEON
          Get off my property or I'll call the
          cops on you!

                    UNCLE RICO
          Go do it then.

                    NAPOLEON
          Maybe I will! Gosh!

INT. NAPOLEON'S KITCHEN - DAY

Napoleon grabs the phone off the hook and
dials.

INT. PEDRO'S HOUSE - DAY

A phone rings. Pedro sits on a couch, he picks
up the phone next to him.

(Intercut with Napoleon in kitchen)

                    PEDRO
        Hello?

                    NAPOLEON
        Pedro? How's it going?

                    PEDRO
        Good.

                    NAPOLEON
        What are you doing right now?

                    PEDRO
        Just relaxing.

                    NAPOLEON
        Deb just called me. She pretty much
        hates me right now.

                    PEDRO
        Why?

                    NAPOLEON
        Cuz my Uncle Rico's an idiot.

                    PEDRO
        Do you have anything you can give her?

                    NAPOLEON
        No. Not unless she likes fish. Are you
        still gonna give a speech tomorrow?

                    PEDRO
        Yeah. Are you going to come?

                    NAPOLEON
        Yes. I'll be there. Do you already
        know what you're gonna say?

                    PEDRO
         Yeah, but not all of it.

                  NAPOLEON
         Just tell them that . . . Their
         wildest dreams will come true if they
         vote for you.

Pedro takes a deep breath. BEAT.

INT. NAPOLEON'S KITCHEN - DAY

Napoleon listens.

                  NAPOLEON
         I'll see you tomorrow Pedro.

Napoleon hangs up the phone. He turns around
and walks to the bay window. He watches Uncle
Rico through the window.

Uncle Rico throws a football and then cusses
himself out.

Napoleon looks on. ZOOM in on Napoleon.

EXT. EMPTY ROAD - MORNING

The sun is popping up over the rolling hills.
BEAT. The school bus drives across frame.

EXT. NAPOLEON'S HOUSE - MORNING

Napoleon wearing a Vote 4 Pedro T-Shirt again,
a Walkman, and carrying a tin-foil wrapped
fish, walks out of his front door. Uncle Rico's
Buick is missing. Napoleon walks to the end of
the driveway and gets on the bus.

INT. SCHOOL BUS - MORNING

Napoleon walks to the back of the bus. He sits
across from Vern.

                              VERN
             What are you listening to Napoleon?

                            NAPOLEON
             None of your business, flip.

Both boys turn toward the windows. Napoleon
picks up the tin-foiled fish and smells it.

INT. HIGH SCHOOL AUDITORIUM - DAY

The entire AUDIENCE is sitting quietly staring
up at an empty stage. Summer Wheatley walks on
to stage and a spotlight follows her. She is
wearing a pant suit.

The Audience cheers for her. Pedro and Napoleon
watch from backstage.

                            SUMMER
             Well, I never thought I'd make it here
             today . . .

EXT. NEIGHBORHOOD STREET - DAY

Uncle Rico walks briskly down the street. He is
wearing his name badge and carrying Bust Plus
pamphlets.

INT. OFFSTAGE ROOM - DAY

Pedro stands nervously wearing a bolo tie and
cowboy boots. He is staring at his crumpled
speech. Napoleon stands next to him.

INT. HIGH SCHOOL AUDITORIUM - DAY

                            SUMMER
             Who wants to eat chimichangas next
             year? Not me . . . With me, it will
             be summer all year round.

(Pronounced chimney-chain-guz)

INT. OFFSTAGE ROOM - DAY

Pedro looks up and mouths the words: Ayúdeme
Señor.

INT. HIGH SCHOOL AUDITORIUM - DAY

The Audience applauds. The principal stands on
stage with a microphone in hand.

                    PRINCIPAL
          And now, Summer will perform her skit
          with some members of the Happy Hands
          Club.

A LOVE SONG can be heard.

INT. OFFSTAGE ROOM - DAY

A TEACHER walks up to Pedro.

                    TEACHER
          You're speech is up next. Your skit
          better be pretty good.

                    PEDRO
          A skit?

                    TEACHER
          You perform a skit after your speech
          Pedro.

                    NAPOLEON
What? A flippin' skit! Why didn't anybody tell
us about this?!

INT. HIGH SCHOOL AUDITORIUM - DAY

Several GIRLS including Summer and Trisha
wearing matching black spandex outfits wave
their hands majestically to a Bryan Adams-type
song. The audience is in awe. The Principal
stands offstage, mesmerized.

INT. REX'S KITCHEN - DAY

Uncle Rico hits casually at a dining table.
STARLA, a thirty something body builder lady,
sits across from Uncle Rico.

Uncle Rico has several pamphlets strewn over
the table. He crosses his legs.

                    UNCLE RICO
          Now if you look right here, we have
          Sally Johnson from Manitou, Colorado.

Uncle Rico hands Starla an opened pamphlet.

                    UNCLE RICO (CONT'D)
          Can you read that testimonial right
          there?

                    STARLA
          Sure, "After using Bust Plus, I have
          such big boobs . . .

Starla chokes on her word.

                    STARLA (CONT'D)
          Um, I don't feel comfortable reading
          this.

                    UNCLE RICO
          That's fine, that's fine, but do you
          feel comfortable with me?

                    STARLA
          Well, this is kind of personal.

                    UNCLE RICO
          Right, well lets get down to the
          point, what size do you take?

                    STARLA
          Um, a B.

                    UNCLE RICO
        How do you feel about that?

INT. HIGH SCHOOL AUDITORIUM - DAY

A CHEERING Audience.

INT. OFFSTAGE ROOM - DAY

Napoleon and Pedro stand frozen in the dressing
room.

                    PEDRO
        I don't really want to be president
        anyway.

                    NAPOLEON
        Pedro just listen to your heart!
        That's what I'd do.

                    PEDRO
        I'll just tell them that I don't have
        nothing to say.

INT. HIGH SCHOOL AUDITORIUM - DAY

Pedro walks out onto the stage. The spotlight
blares him. He holds his speech over his eyes.
Napoleon watches.

Pedro tries to see someone familiar in the
audience. He stumbles and kicks the podium.

                    PEDRO
        Hello, I don't have much to say.

INT. REX'S KITCHEN - DAY

Uncle Rico is standing near a rack of pots and
pans. Starla is sitting petrified.

                    UNCLE RICO
          Now, lets just say . . .

Uncle Rico, attempting to be graceful, pulls
two small cooking pots off the rack.

                UNCLE RICO (CONT'D)
          . . . You are somewhere around here.

Uncle Rico places the small pots up to his
chest.

EXT. REX'S HOUSE - DAY

Rex of Rex-Kwon-Do gets out of a Subaru Brat.
He is in his hammer pants and a polo. He walks
toward the house.

INT. REX'S KITCHEN - DAY

Uncle Rico has the pots up to his chest still.

                    UNCLE RICO
          With three weeks of my product you're
          gonna be about here.

Uncle Rico grabs two larger pots from the rack
and proceeds to hold them over Starla's chest.
DOOR SLAM.

Rex appears. Uncle Rico, frozen, looks back at
him.

INT. HIGH SCHOOL AUDITORIUM - DAY

Pedro is still at the microphone. His forehead
is sweaty. He wipes it.

                      PEDRO
          . . . a great FFA schedule lined
          up . . . and I'd like to see more of
          that.

EXT. REX'S HOUSE - DAY

SOUNDS of pots crashing, and Uncle Rico getting
beat up.

INT. OFFSTAGE ROOM - DAY

Napoleon looks around, he scratches his head.
Beat. He pulls out a cassette tape from his
Walkman. He looks down at it. Beat. He looks
out towards the stage.

INT. HIGH SCHOOL AUDITORIUM - DAY

Pedro still stands giving his speech.

                    PEDRO
        If you vote for me, all of your wildest
        dreams will come true. Thank you.

The Audience claps less energetically. Pedro
walks backstage.

INT. BACKSTAGE - DAY

Napoleon stands offstage watching Pedro walk
past him. Pedro looks exhausted. He is pulling
off his bolo-tie and unbuttoning his collar.
Napoleon looks at him, lets out a deep breath
and walks away.

                    PRINCIPAL
        And now we will enjoy a skit by Pedro
        Sanchez.

The curtains open to an empty stage. Silence.
BEAT. The Audience looks on. Napoleon slowly
walks out on stage.

INT. SOUND ROOM - DAY

A SOUND TECHNICIAN puts the cassette into a
tape player. He hits play.

INT. HIGH SCHOOL AUDITORIUM - DAY

Napoleon turns and faces the Audience with his
hands in his pockets. Beat. DANCE MUSIC begins.

The DANCE MUSIC's beat increases.

In sync with the beats, Napoleon begins to
dance.

The Audience is SILENT.

Napoleon dances seamlessly for the entire song.
He struts a fusion of disco and hip-hop dance
moves. It is amazing.

The song finishes and Napoleon runs off,
leaving an empty stage. Beat. The Audience
erupts with APPLAUSE.

INT. OFFSTAGE ROOM - DAY

Pedro stands smiling.

INT. HIGH SCHOOL AUDITORIUM - DAY

Don, Summer, and Trisha sit in the audience,
stunned and motionless.

Deb sits further down and she smiles broadly,
clapping furiously.

EXT. MAIN STREET - DAY

Napoleon walks down the street by himself.
MUSIC plays.

EXT. BUS STATION - DAY

Kip and LaFawnduh stand at a bus station. Kip is carrying two suitcases. A bus pulls up. The destination card reads DETROIT.

Napoleon stands across the street and sees them.

Kip and LaFawnduh step onto the bus.

Napoleon looks on. The bus pulls away.

EXT. AIRSTREAM - DAY

The bus wipes passed to reveal Uncle Rico standing in front of his Airstream trailer throwing a football with his left arm. His right arm is in a sling. He struggles to throw a football towards a video camera on a tripod. He squints in frustration, lets out a sigh. He notices something out in the distance.

A PRETTY LADY rides a bike towards him on a dirt road.

He goes for the football.

She gets closer, he winds up, and waits. She looks over at him from the bike.

He throws the foot ball as tough as he can.

A bike tire skids to a stop. Uncle Rico turns to her. She glances back.

                    UNCLE RICO
          Wanna see my video?

EXT. PARK - DAY

A white tres-leches cake reads in frosting:
Presidente Pedro! Felicidades! A piece is
pulled out.

Pedro stands behind a picnic table full of
food, he is surrounded by family members,
Cholos #1 and #2, they all eat cake and pat him
on the back. He brings a big piece of cake up
to his mouth and bites it.

EXT. NAPOLEON'S HOUSE - DAY

Tina the llama eats food from a hand. Grandma
stands on the other side of the fence feeding
and petting her.

EXT. HIGH SCHOOL BASKETBALL COURT - DAY

Napoleon is alone playing tether-ball. His
Walkman and tin-foiled fish are on the ground.

Deb walks up. Napoleon stops. They look at each
other.

                    NAPOLEON
          I caught you a delicious bass.

Deb smiles at Napoleon.

                    NAPOLEON (CONT'D)
          Wanna play me?

Deb smiles. Napoleon swings her the tether
ball. They play tether ball as the camera
slowly ZOOMS OUT.

                              FADE OUT: